Colourpedia
ANIMALS

Discover fantastic facts
as you colour!

ARCTURUS

HOW TO USE THIS BOOK

Throughout the book you'll find lots of amazing animal illustrations to colour. Also included are guide photographs, like this, which show what these animals look like in real life.

You can follow these real-life colours, or pick totally different ones and let your imagination run wild.

Turn the page to begin!

ARCTURUS

This edition published in 2019 by Arcturus Publishing Limited
26/27 Bickels Yard, 151–153 Bermondsey Street,
London SE1 3HA

Written by Julia Adams
Illustrated by Lindsey Leigh, with additional illustrations © Shutterstock.
Designed by Ariadne Ward
Edited by Susannah Bailey
Photos © Shutterstock

ISBN: 978-1-78428-807-5
CH005747UK
Supplier 29 Date 0519 Print run 8743

Printed in China

CONTENTS

Chapter 1: Animal Antics

LET'S GO!

The animal kingdom is a harsh place, where every day is a fight for survival. In this chapter, we look at the amazing instincts that help creatures to stay alive. First up is migration—when animals travel huge distances for part of the year.

Common terns have some of the longest migrations of all birds. Every summer, they breed in the northern countries of Europe, North America, and Asia, before flying south to Africa, Southeast Asia, or South America.

Every year, **leatherback turtles** cover huge distances to swim to warm tropical waters. Here, the females crawl onto land to lay their eggs on sandy beaches.

Each autumn, **monarch butterflies** in North America travel southward from the US/Canadian border to escape the cold weather. They can cover distances of up to 4,800 km (3,000 mi)!

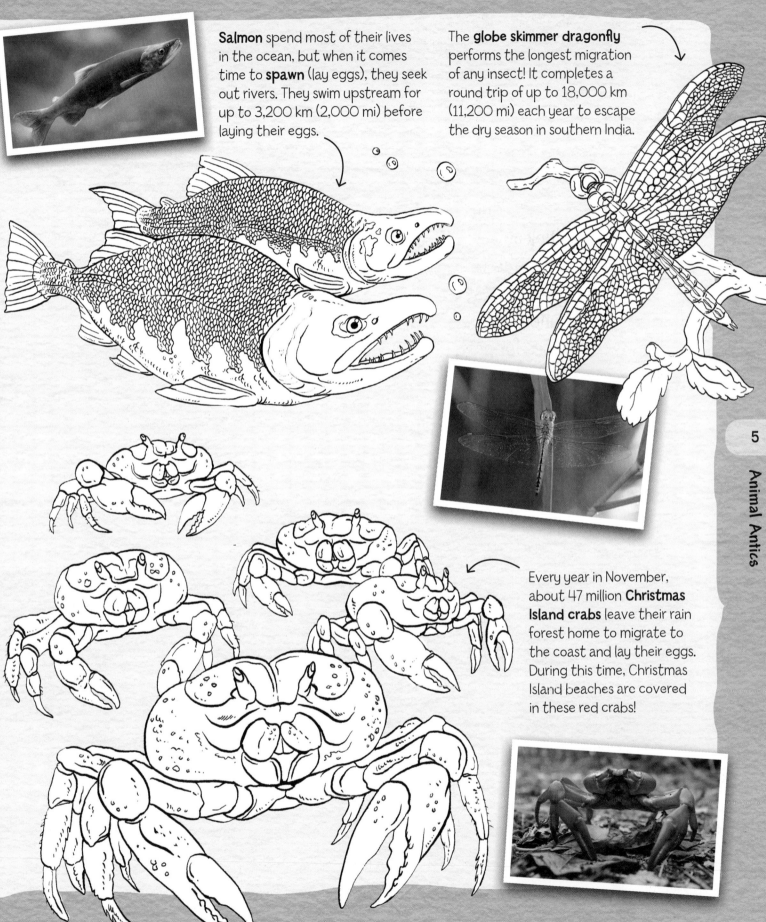

Salmon spend most of their lives in the ocean, but when it comes time to **spawn** (lay eggs), they seek out rivers. They swim upstream for up to 3,200 km (2,000 mi) before laying their eggs.

The **globe skimmer dragonfly** performs the longest migration of any insect! It completes a round trip of up to 18,000 km (11,200 mi) each year to escape the dry season in southern India.

Every year in November, about 47 million **Christmas Island crabs** leave their rain forest home to migrate to the coast and lay their eggs. During this time, Christmas Island beaches are covered in these red crabs!

FIERCE HUNTERS

Meet the predators! These are animals that hunt and kill other creatures for food. They have to be quick, smart, and powerful to successfully catch their meals and avoid going hungry.

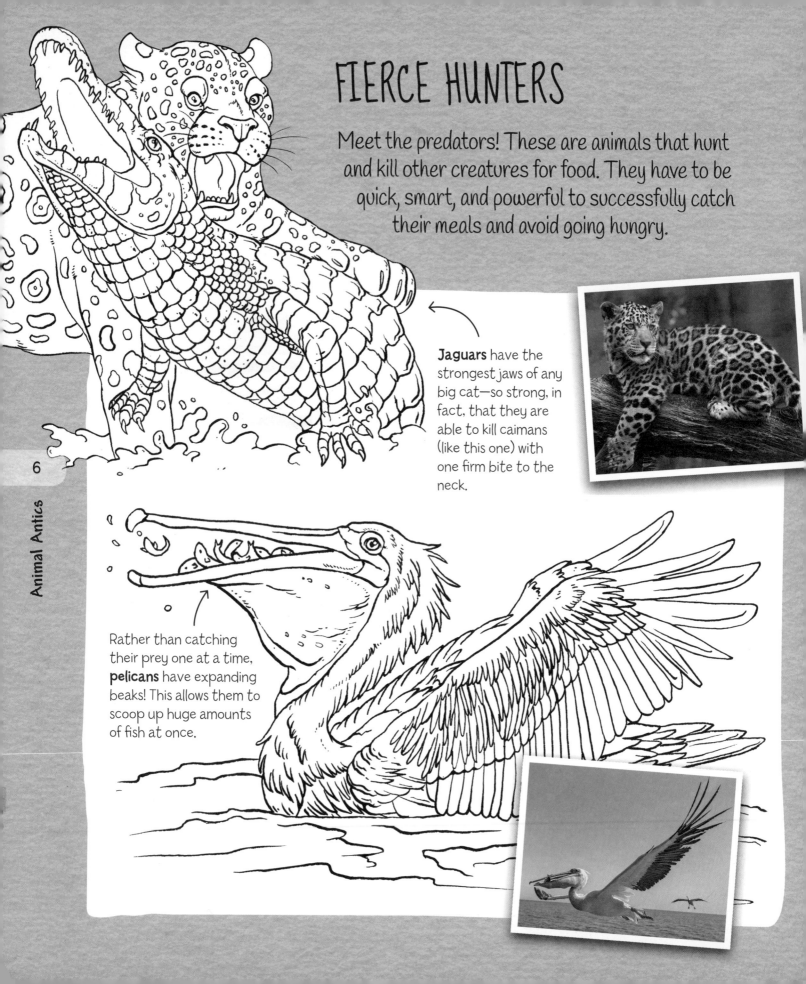

Jaguars have the strongest jaws of any big cat—so strong, in fact, that they are able to kill caimans (like this one) with one firm bite to the neck.

Rather than catching their prey one at a time, **pelicans** have expanding beaks! This allows them to scoop up huge amounts of fish at once.

The **praying mantis** looks a lot like the plants it lives on. Disguised, it lies in wait, pouncing at lightning speed once its target is close enough ...

Peregrine falcons catch their prey by plummeting down from the sky at eye-watering speeds. They pounce on unsuspecting pigeons at up to 320 kph (200 mph)!

The **boa constrictor** uses its long, muscular body to wrap itself firmly around its prey and suffocate it. Because boas don't have any molars to help chew food, their victims are swallowed whole.

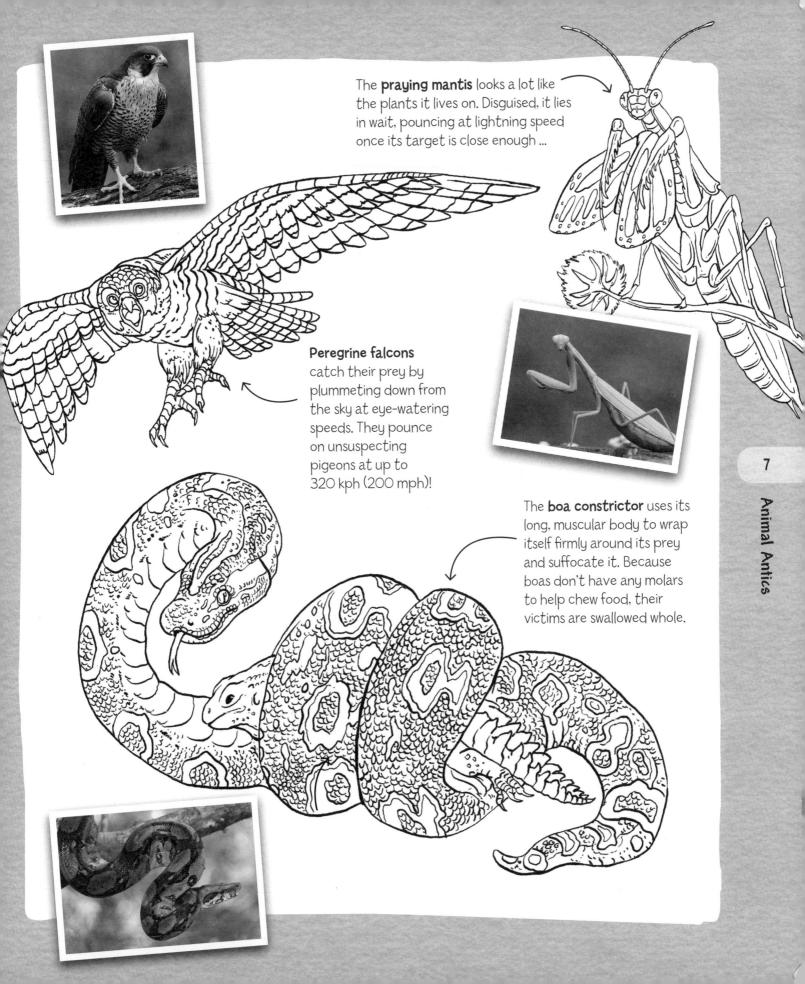

BEASTLY BUFFET

Rather than hunting down their food, many animals know exactly where to go for their meals. Their bodies are often adapted to their way of feeding, too.

Bees fly from flower to flower, using their long tongues to reach the sweet, sticky nectar. They can also let other bees in their hive know about where food is by performing a "waggle dance."

The **giant panda** only eats one type of plant: bamboo. It lives in bamboo forests and has especially large, flat molars to help it crush the stems and leaves.

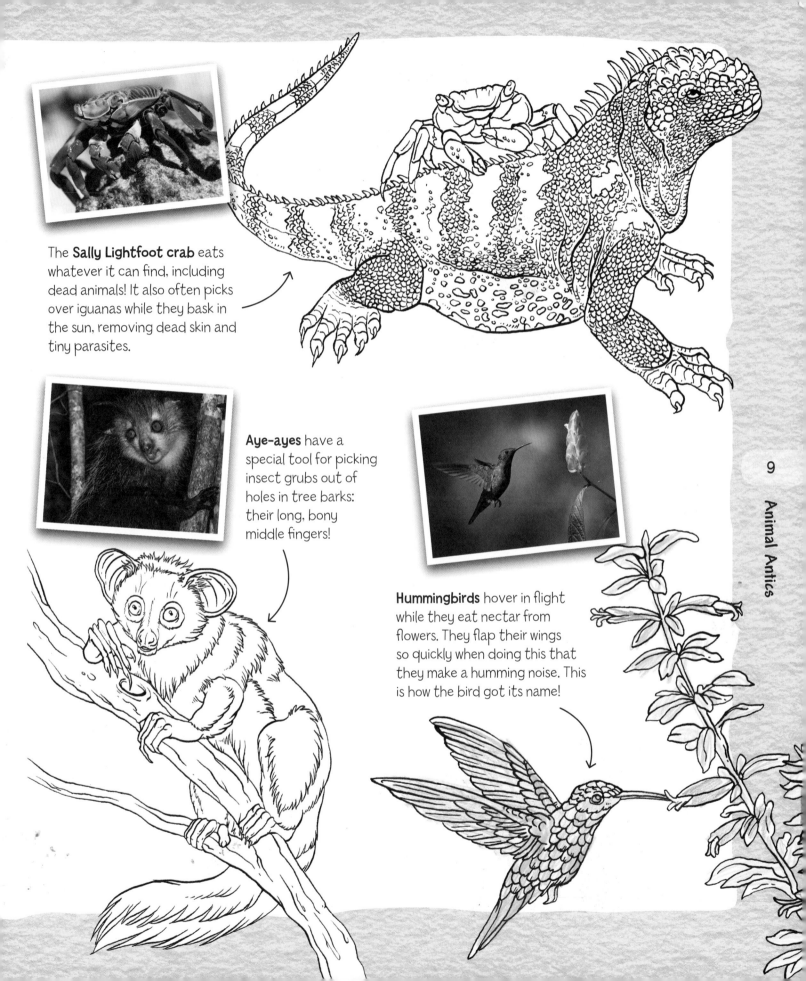

The **Sally Lightfoot crab** eats whatever it can find, including dead animals! It also often picks over iguanas while they bask in the sun, removing dead skin and tiny parasites.

Aye-ayes have a special tool for picking insect grubs out of holes in tree barks: their long, bony middle fingers!

Hummingbirds hover in flight while they eat nectar from flowers. They flap their wings so quickly when doing this that they make a humming noise. This is how the bird got its name!

SPECIAL CEREMONIES

During mating season, male animals will often compete for the attention of females. Their efforts can result in spectacular displays!

Many frogs, such as the **marbled reed frog**, try to attract females with mating calls. Their expanded throats act like a loudspeaker, helping their calls to travel farther.

Great crested grebes perform an elaborate and eye-catching water dance with their mates.

Male **stag flies** use their long horns to battle with each other during mating season. They each try to claim the grounds where females will soon arrive in search of a mate.

Every year, **gemsboks** gather at a mating site called a **lek**. Males lock their horns to fight over who is allowed to be in this space, while the females choose their mate.

Great frigate bird males group together to puff up and show off their huge, red throat pouches. Females then pick the most appealing male.

BRINGING UP BABIES

Some animal parents go to great lengths to help their young survive and get them ready for adult life.

The **kangaroo** is part of a group of mammals called **marsupials**. Marsupials are known for carrying their babies in pouches.

Meerkats teach their young how to hunt, kill, and eat venomous scorpions. They prepare the scorpions by removing the sting, then let the babies pounce on them!

When they are born, **crocodile** young are vulnerable, so their mother protects them by carrying them in her jaws. Crocodile mothers can carry up to 15 young in their mouth at one time!

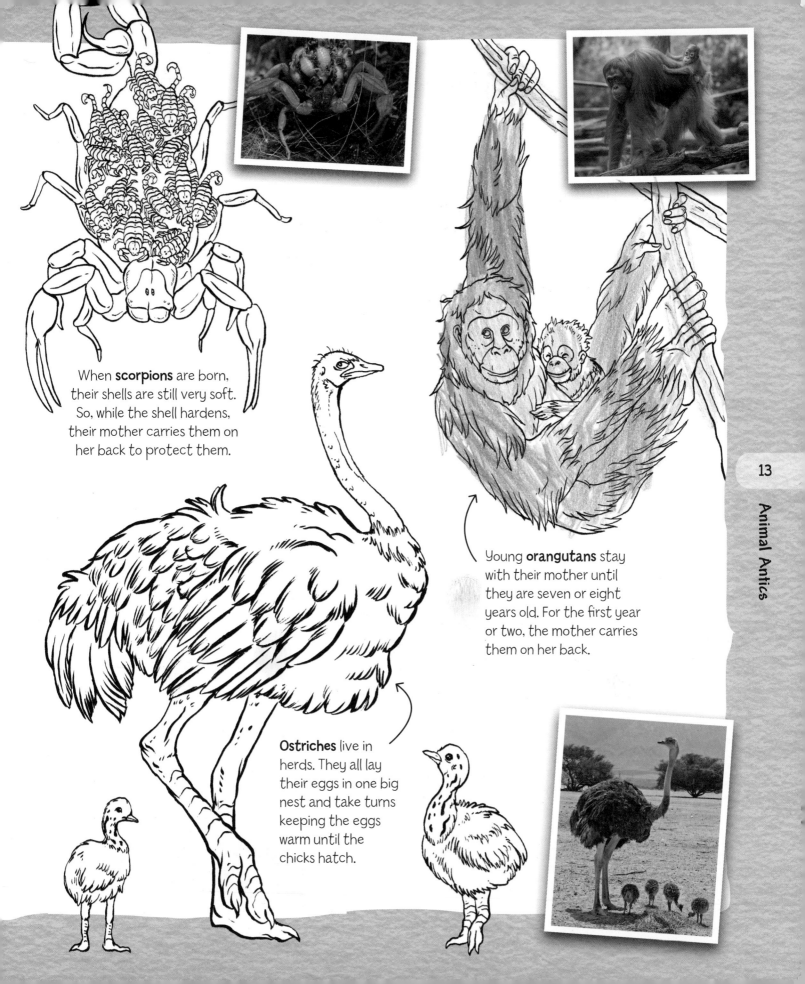

When **scorpions** are born, their shells are still very soft. So, while the shell hardens, their mother carries them on her back to protect them.

Young **orangutans** stay with their mother until they are seven or eight years old. For the first year or two, the mother carries them on her back.

Ostriches live in herds. They all lay their eggs in one big nest and take turns keeping the eggs warm until the chicks hatch.

BETTER TOGETHER

For animals, there are many advantages to being in a group—it keeps them safe from predators, makes hunting easier, and helps when seeking a mate.

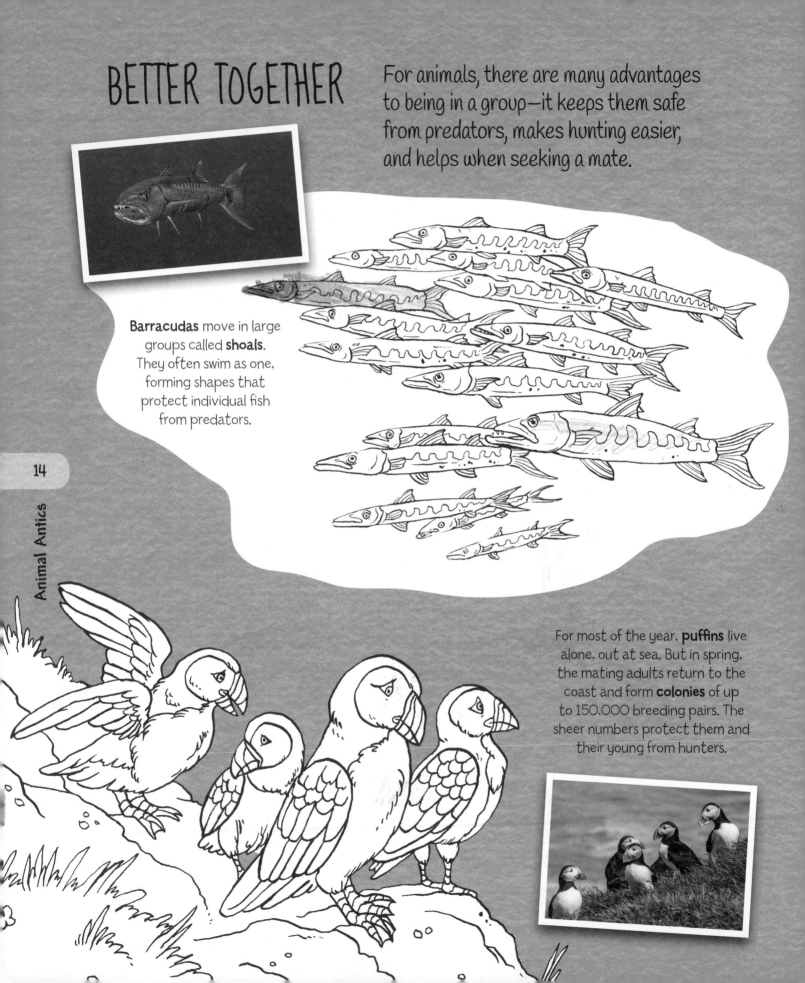

Barracudas move in large groups called **shoals**. They often swim as one, forming shapes that protect individual fish from predators.

For most of the year, **puffins** live alone, out at sea. But in spring, the mating adults return to the coast and form **colonies** of up to 150,000 breeding pairs. The sheer numbers protect them and their young from hunters.

Wolves live and hunt in **packs**. Once they locate their prey, the pack will follow it from a distance, staying out of sight until they're ready to attack.

Mustangs are wild horses. They live in **herds** that have intricate rules. Each member knows its place and how to behave, which makes the herd a strong unit.

MASTER BUILDERS

A creature's home is its shelter. Here, it can hide from danger, raise its young, and sleep undisturbed. Meet some of nature's most skilled architects!

Oropendolas weave elaborate hanging nests that can be up to 2 m (6.5 ft) long. They breed in colonies of up to 100 pairs of birds, with each of their nests hanging off the same tree!

The **golden eagle** builds a large nest for its chicks called an **aerie**, or **eyrie**. It is usually perched high up on a cliff or a tree and used every year. Each nesting bird will add to the structure, which means that some aeries can be over 4 m (13 ft) deep!

Paper wasps build their complex homes by chewing wood and turning it into paper pulp. Once the pulp has dried, the nest is sturdy and water resistant.

The **badger** uses its powerful paws and long claws to dig its home, which is called a **den**, or sett. Well-built dens are sometimes used by badger families for hundreds of years!

ON GUARD!

Many creatures have to defend themselves from predators on a daily basis. The more successful they are, the more likely it is that they'll survive.

With their bright skin patterns, **poison dart frogs** are sending a warning: They are highly toxic. Some have skin that is so poisonous, one frog could kill 10 people!

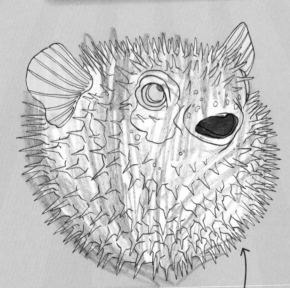

If a **skunk** feels threatened, it will give a brief warning before spraying a nasty-smelling fluid from just below its tail. It can aim at attackers that are up to 4 m (13 ft) away!

Like the puffer fish, the **porcupine fish** can suck in water and expand into a ball shape. Its long spikes make it even more difficult for predators to attack.

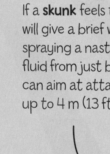

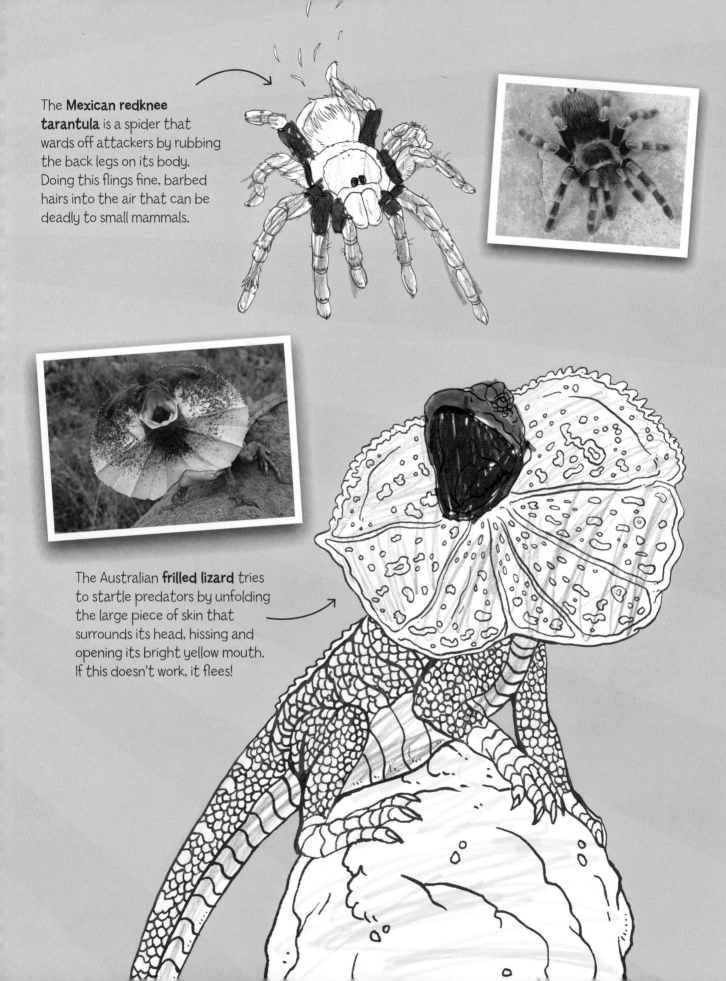

The **Mexican redknee tarantula** is a spider that wards off attackers by rubbing the back legs on its body. Doing this flings fine, barbed hairs into the air that can be deadly to small mammals.

The Australian **frilled lizard** tries to startle predators by unfolding the large piece of skin that surrounds its head, hissing and opening its bright yellow mouth. If this doesn't work, it flees!

MIGHTY MAMMALS

Read about all the different animals that make up our animal kingdom! First up, mammals—creatures that produce milk for their young and often have fur.

There are many kinds of **antelopes** around the world. They all have hooves and horns, and can run incredibly fast.

Koalas live in Australia. They are great climbers, and the only food they eat is eucalyptus leaves!

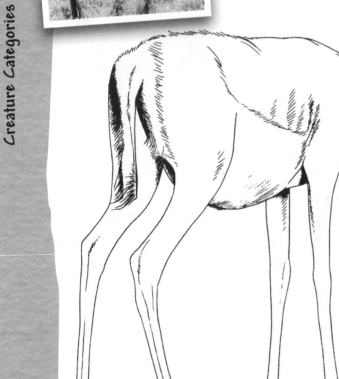

Fox mothers give birth to between two and 12 cubs every year. Together, they make up a litter. Imagine having 11 brothers and sisters!

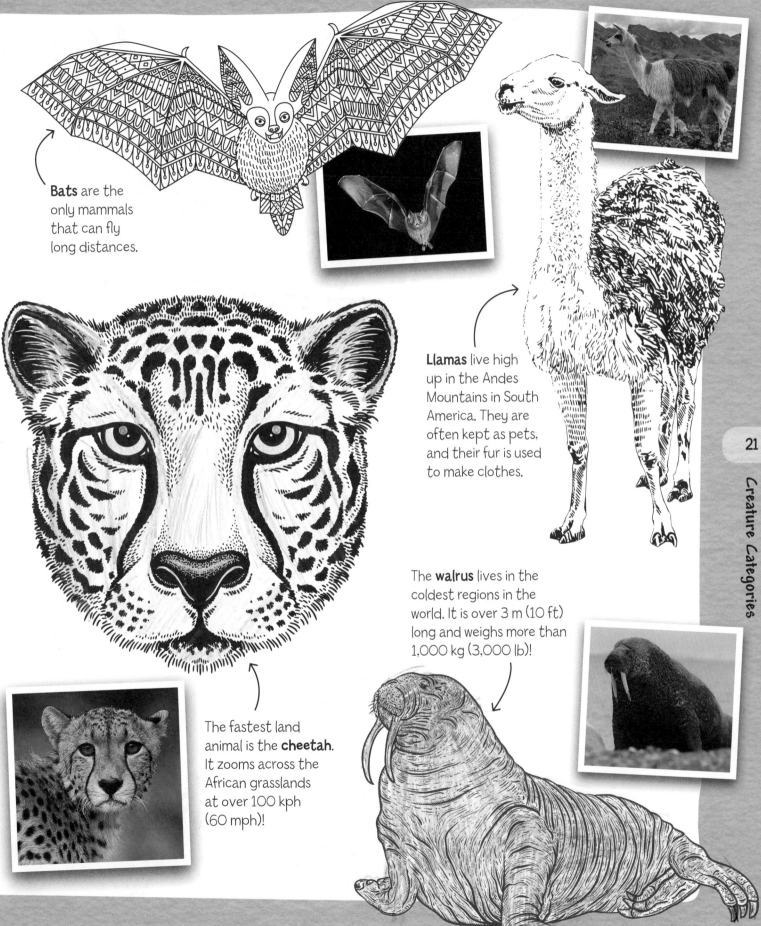

Bats are the only mammals that can fly long distances.

Llamas live high up in the Andes Mountains in South America. They are often kept as pets, and their fur is used to make clothes.

The **walrus** lives in the coldest regions in the world. It is over 3 m (10 ft) long and weighs more than 1,000 kg (3,000 lb)!

The fastest land animal is the **cheetah**. It zooms across the African grasslands at over 100 kph (60 mph)!

BEAUTIFUL BIRDS

Most birds can fly. Their light bodies and strong wings help them soar into the sky, and they sometimes stay there for hours. They lay eggs, from which their chicks hatch after a few weeks.

Hawks are large, powerful birds of prey. Their wingspan (distance between the tips of the wings) is about 1 m (40 in).

Get your pencils ready! The **golden pheasant** is covered in eye-catching feathers and loads of patterns!

There are hundreds of different kinds of **finches** around the world. The shape of their beak depends on which foods they eat.

Flamingos live together in large groups, or flocks. When they are resting, they often stand on one leg.

The **toucan** uses its impressive beak to pick and peel fruit before eating it.

This is a male **duck**, or **drake**. Ducks can often be seen with their heads in the water and tails in the air, while they forage for food.

REMARKABLE REPTILES

Covered in scales and sometimes even tough shells, reptiles often live in hot areas. This is because a lot of them need the sun to keep warm.

Alligators live by the water and are very strong swimmers. They hunt with their powerful jaws and razor-sharp teeth.

When a **cobra** feels threatened, it will raise its head and fan out the top part of its body. This is to scare off attackers.

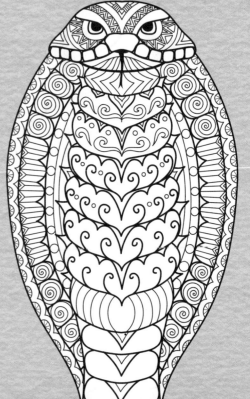

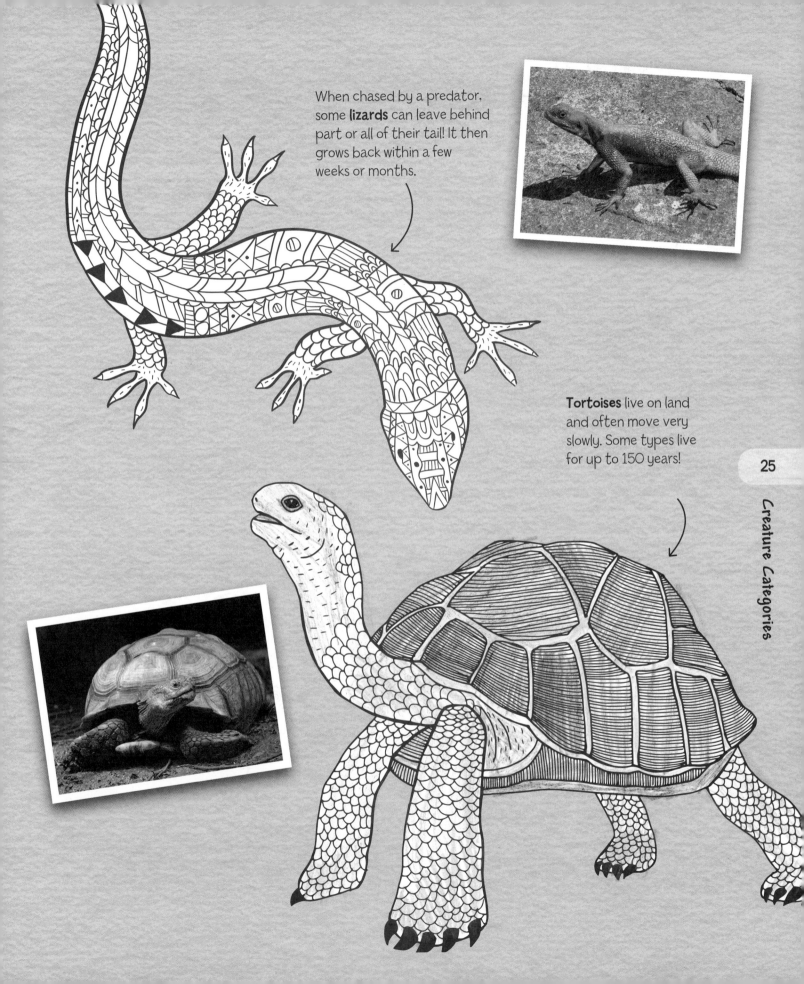

When chased by a predator, some **lizards** can leave behind part or all of their tail! It then grows back within a few weeks or months.

Tortoises live on land and often move very slowly. Some types live for up to 150 years!

AMAZING AMPHIBIANS

When they start life, amphibians are called larvae and only live in the water. Once they become mature, they move onto land, but often stay close to their first home.

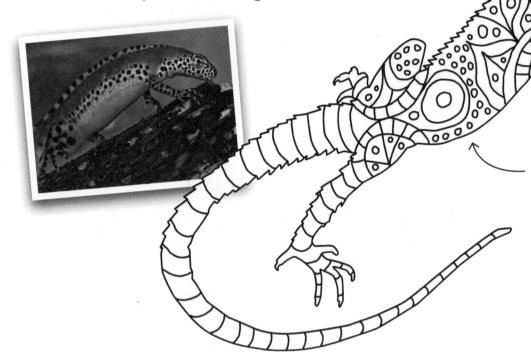

Many **newts** find shelter and go into a deep sleep every winter. This is called **hibernation**, and it protects the animals from the cold.

Unlike most amphibians, **toads** have dry, leathery skin and can live far away from water.

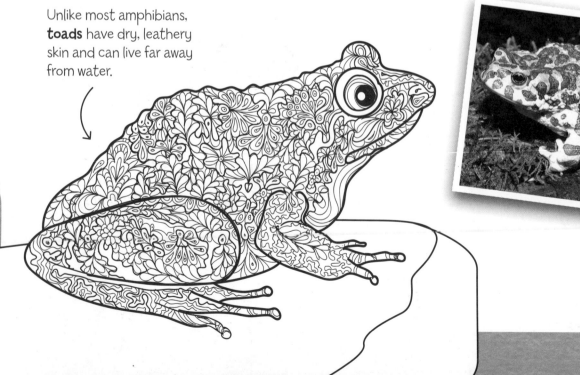

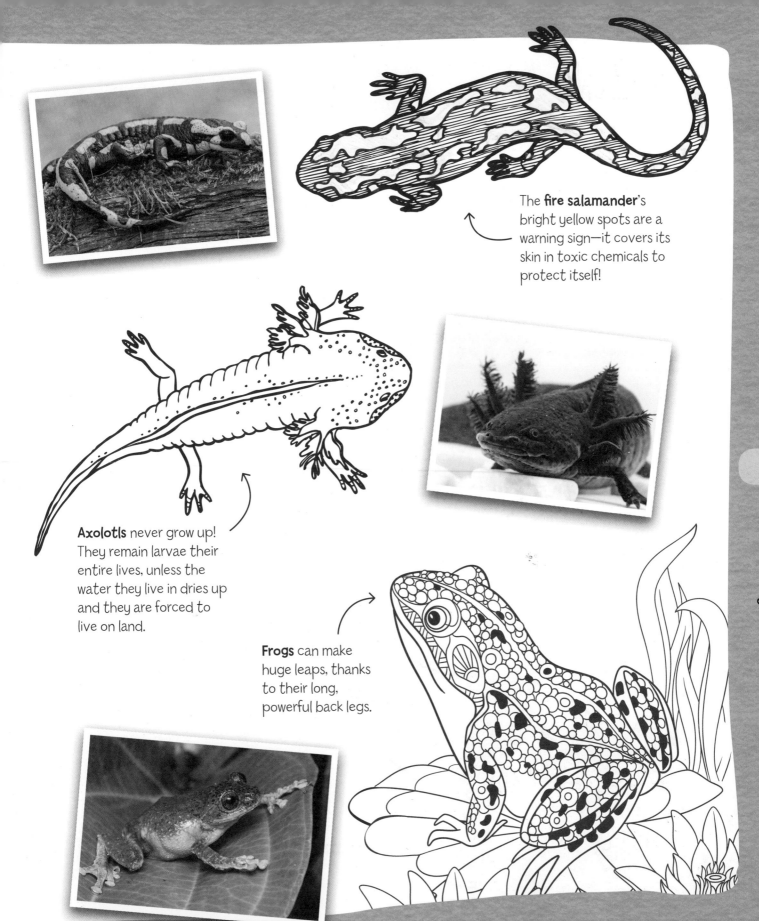

The **fire salamander**'s bright yellow spots are a warning sign—it covers its skin in toxic chemicals to protect itself!

Axolotls never grow up! They remain larvae their entire lives, unless the water they live in dries up and they are forced to live on land.

Frogs can make huge leaps, thanks to their long, powerful back legs.

Creature Categories

SOMETHING FISHY

Fish live underwater, using gills to breathe and fins to swim. They can be found in all kinds of places—from icy lakes to tropical oceans.

The dramatic-looking **Siamese fighting fish** live up to their name: The males are often very aggressive toward each other!

Although **flying fish** can't actually fly, they can use their wing-shaped fins to make long, gliding leaps above the water's surface.

The shimmering, sleek body of the **tuna** is built for speed and endurance. It is one of the most powerful swimmers in the ocean.

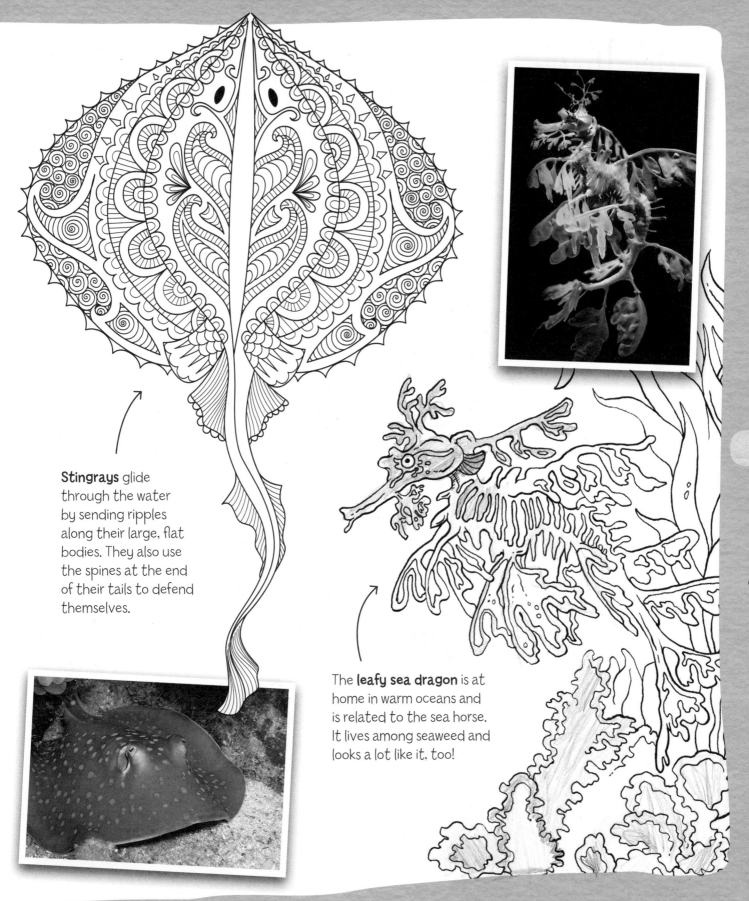

Stingrays glide through the water by sending ripples along their large, flat bodies. They also use the spines at the end of their tails to defend themselves.

The **leafy sea dragon** is at home in warm oceans and is related to the sea horse. It lives among seaweed and looks a lot like it, too!

BUGS BIG AND SMALL

We sometimes call insects "bugs." They are often small, but there are many of them—for every human on the planet, there are more than 200 million insects!

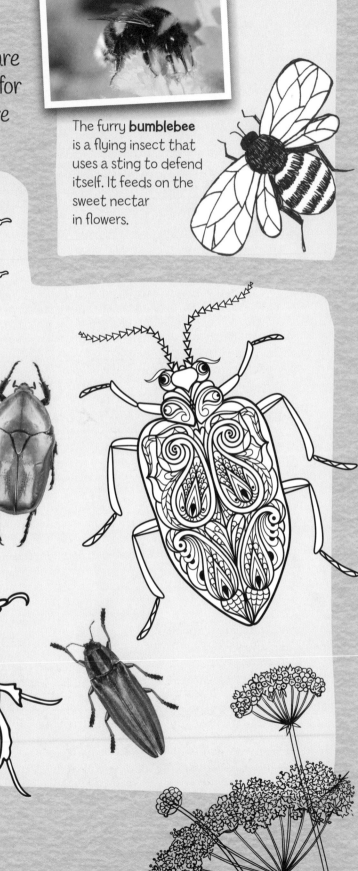

The furry **bumblebee** is a flying insect that uses a sting to defend itself. It feeds on the sweet nectar in flowers.

Beetles are little six-legged creatures whose bodies are protected by shells. These shells are often covered in eye-catching patterns.

The **butterfly** starts life as a caterpillar. It then transforms in a **chrysalis** into its beautiful, winged, adult form.

Flies can't chew food. Therefore they have to throw up digestive enzymes onto what they want to eat, and then slurp it back up when it softens!

Moths have a similar life cycle to butterflies. As adults, they are often **nocturnal** (most active at night).

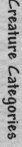

31

CRAWLING ARACHNIDS

All arachnids have eight legs, and their body is split into two parts—the head and the thorax. Arachnids use two pincers attached to their head to help them eat their prey.

Many **spiders** catch their prey in complex spiderwebs. The silk that spiders use to weave these webs is one of the strongest materials in nature.

Creature Categories

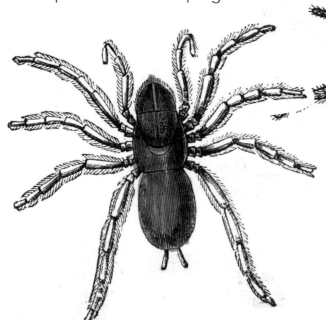

Most spiders have eight eyes!

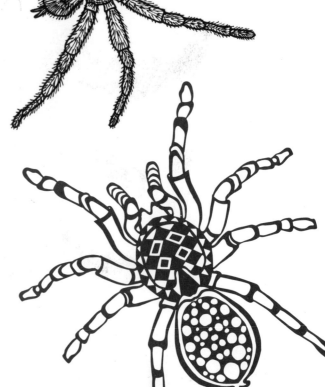

Spiders often catch prey through **ambush**. This means that they lie in wait until an animal is close enough for them to pounce.

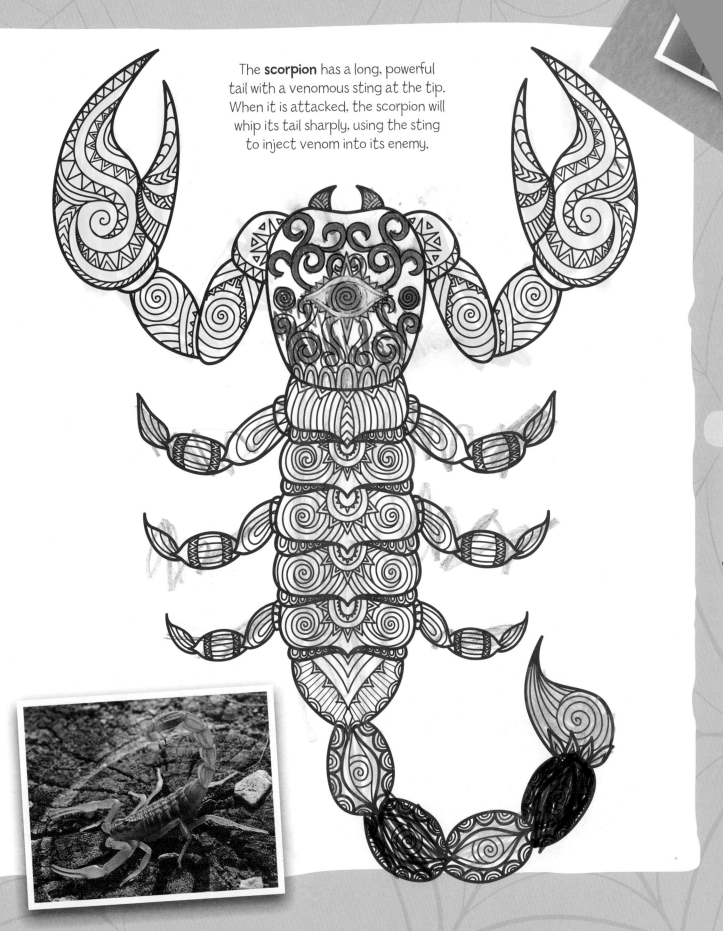

The **scorpion** has a long, powerful tail with a venomous sting at the tip. When it is attacked, the scorpion will whip its tail sharply, using the sting to inject venom into its enemy.

SOFTLY DOES IT

Because they have no bones, soft-bodied animals are incredibly flexible but also very vulnerable.

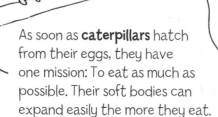

As soon as **caterpillars** hatch from their eggs, they have one mission: To eat as much as possible. Their soft bodies can expand easily the more they eat.

Octopuses can be huge, but their soft bodies allow them to fit into the tiniest of spaces. For example, a 270 kg (600 lb) octopus can fit into a tube that is 2.5 cm (1 in) wide!

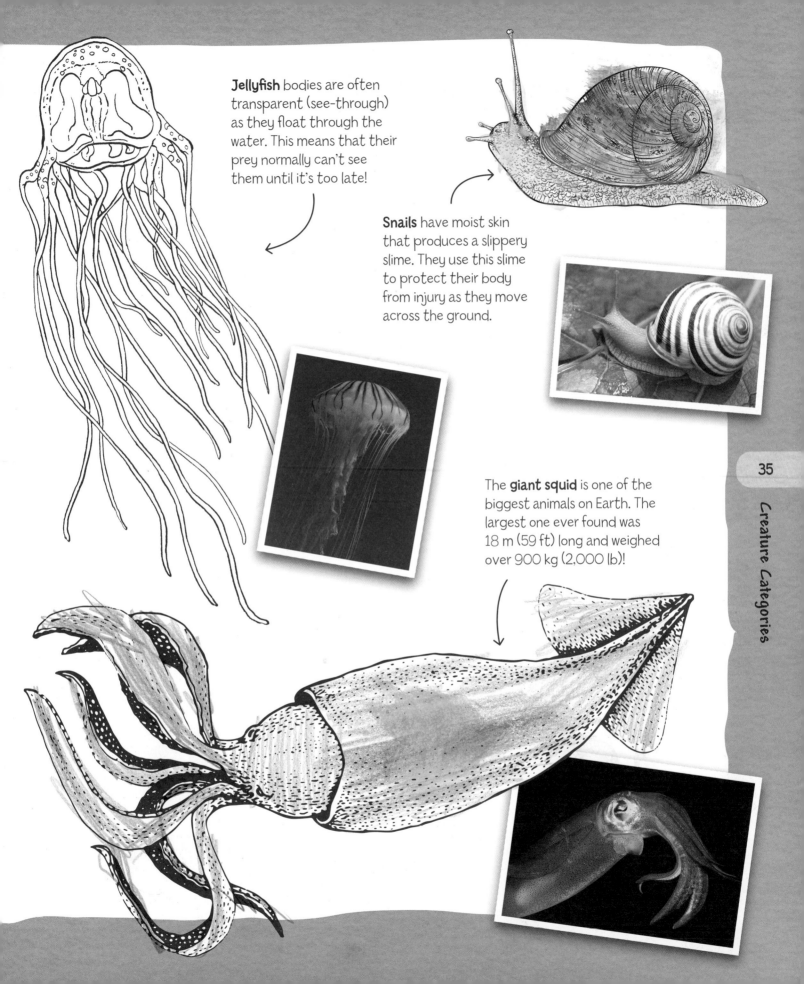

Jellyfish bodies are often transparent (see-through) as they float through the water. This means that their prey normally can't see them until it's too late!

Snails have moist skin that produces a slippery slime. They use this slime to protect their body from injury as they move across the ground.

The **giant squid** is one of the biggest animals on Earth. The largest one ever found was 18 m (59 ft) long and weighed over 900 kg (2,000 lb)!

THE COLD POLES

Where do different animals live? Let's start by learning who has settled in the chilliest regions on Earth—the North and South Poles.

Orcas live in the icy waters of the Arctic (North Pole) and Antarctic (South Pole). They have a thick layer of fat, called blubber, that sits under their skin and keeps them warm.

Sea eagles catch their prey by plunging toward the surface of the ocean with outstretched feet. They use their large talons (claws) to grab unsuspecting fish.

For many months of the year, **polar bears** live and hunt on the ice shelves of the North Pole.

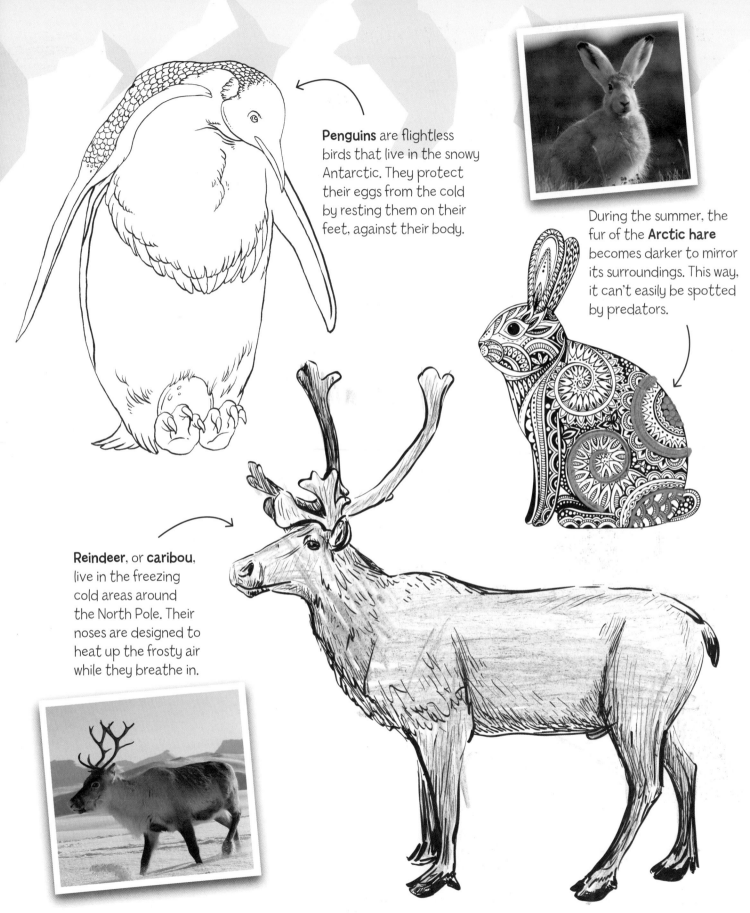

Penguins are flightless birds that live in the snowy Antarctic. They protect their eggs from the cold by resting them on their feet, against their body.

During the summer, the fur of the **Arctic hare** becomes darker to mirror its surroundings. This way, it can't easily be spotted by predators.

Reindeer, or **caribou**, live in the freezing cold areas around the North Pole. Their noses are designed to heat up the frosty air while they breathe in.

SCORCHING DESERTS

With temperatures of around 50°C (125°F) during the day and hardly any rain, the desert is a tough place to survive.

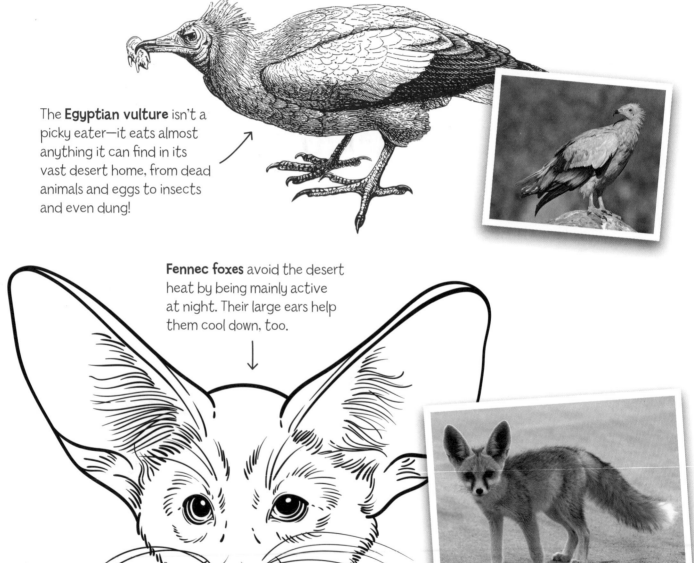

The **Egyptian vulture** isn't a picky eater—it eats almost anything it can find in its vast desert home, from dead animals and eggs to insects and even dung!

Fennec foxes avoid the desert heat by being mainly active at night. Their large ears help them cool down, too.

Roadrunners are tough predators. They hunt, kill, and eat venomous rattlesnakes!

The **rattlesnake** got its name because of the noise it makes when it is under attack. It shakes its tail, which is made up of hard, loose segments that knock together and rattle!

The hump of the **dromedary** (Arabian camel) stores fat. Its body can break this fat down into energy and water if the camel can't find any in its surroundings.

LUSH RAIN FORESTS

The forests in hot, wet parts of the world are called rain forests. They are full of wildlife, much of which has yet to be discovered!

Basilisk lizards have an amazing skill: They can walk on water! They run upright across the water's surface for 4.5 m (15 ft) or more.

Tree frogs have sticky pads on their feet that help them cling to any surface—even the underside of leaves!

The **proboscis monkey**'s calls echo through its long, bulbous nose. This makes the sounds louder and helps them travel farther.

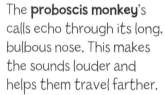

The wings of **blue morpho butterflies** are a shiny blue on the outside. When they fold their wings up, only the brown underside shows.

The **macaw**'s strong, hooked beak helps it crack the shells of nuts and seeds.

Red-bellied piranhas have razor-sharp teeth. They live in shoals and only attack if they feel threatened.

The **capybara** is about as large as a medium-sized dog. It is the world's largest rodent.

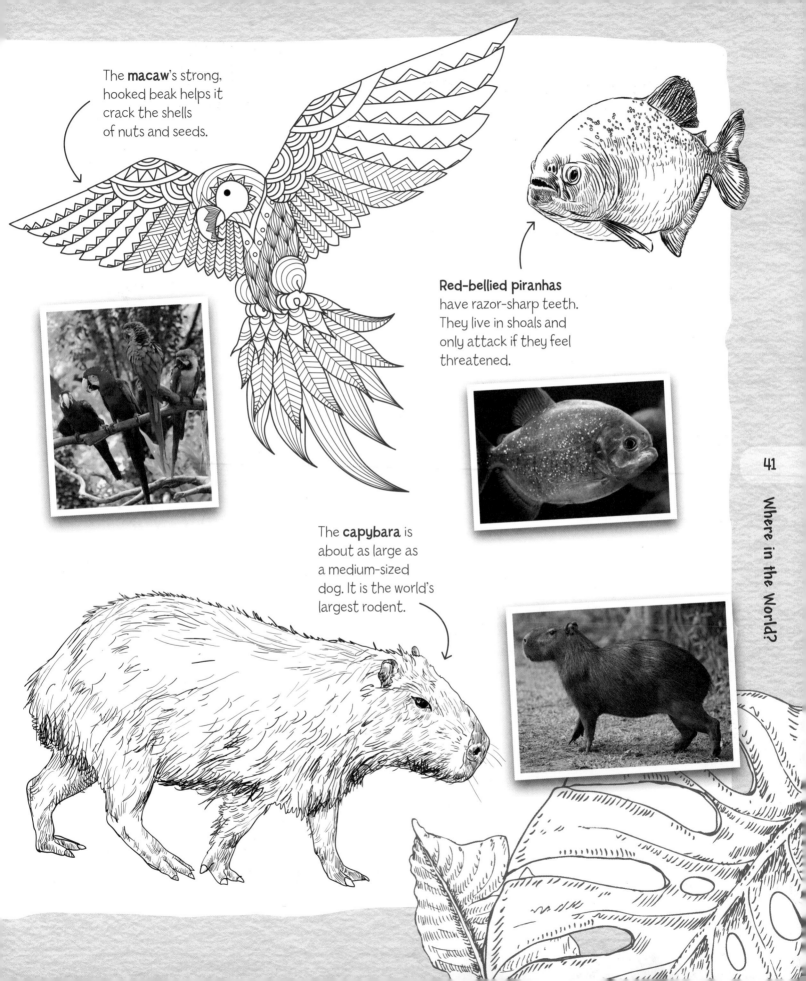

VAST OCEANS

Over half of our planet is covered in water. Beneath the crashing waves of the world's oceans exists a huge underwater world, full of wondrous animals.

Scallops move by sucking in water and then pushing it out with great force, propelling themselves forward.

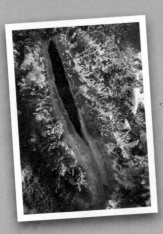

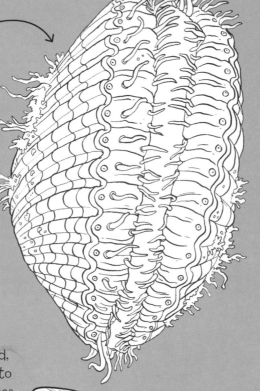

Have you ever found a **shell** on the beach? Each shell used to be the home of a soft-bodied animal called a **mollusk**, or **mollusc**. When the animal dies, its shell gets washed to shore.

When a **puffer fish** gets attacked, it quickly swallows enough water to blow itself up into a ball. This makes it very tricky for predators to eat it.

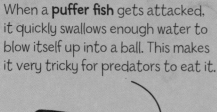

Where in the World?

Sea turtles need to come to the water's surface to breathe. However, they can hold their breath for a very long time—some for up to five hours!

The **sea horse** uses its long, coiled tail to hold on to seaweed and kelp in strong currents.

Anemones look like flowers, but they are animals. The hole in the middle is their mouth!

If a **starfish** loses any of its five arms, it can grow them back again!

FEELING FRESH

Rivers, waterfalls, and lakes are all fed by freshwater and provide a home for creatures great and small—whether they live in the water or along the banks.

River otters often use tools to get to their food. They smash shells by using rocks as hammers.

Catfish use the barbels (whiskers) on either side of their mouth to find food.

Brown bears catch salmon from rivers as the salmon swim upstream to mate.

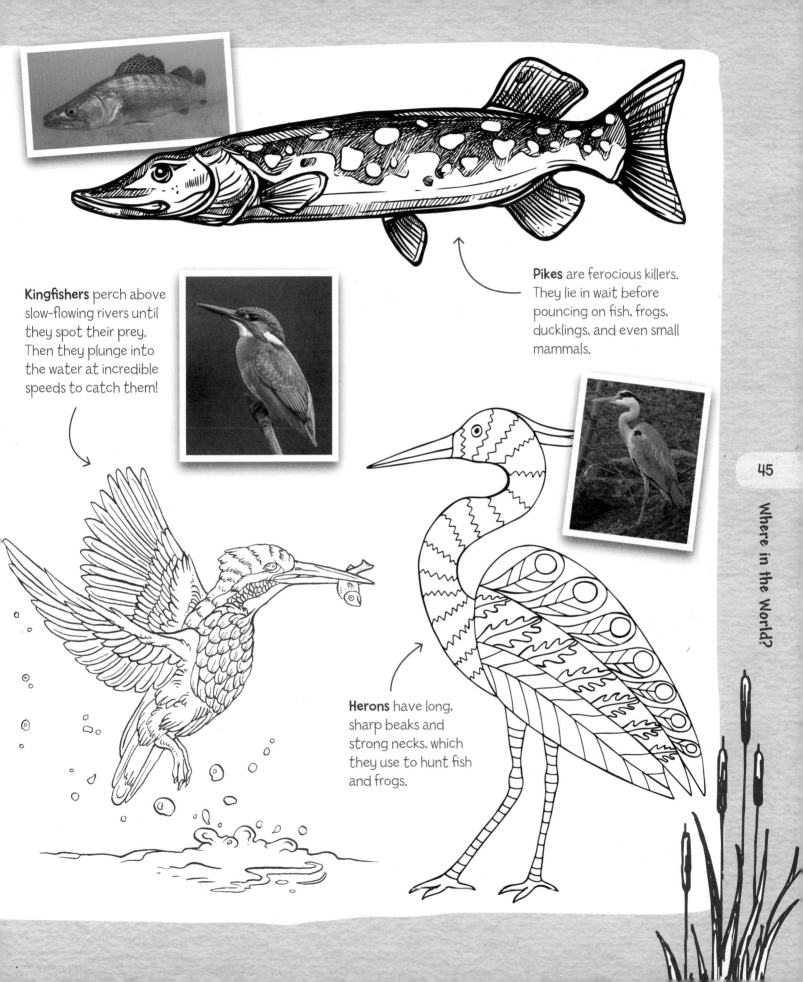

Kingfishers perch above slow-flowing rivers until they spot their prey. Then they plunge into the water at incredible speeds to catch them!

Pikes are ferocious killers. They lie in wait before pouncing on fish, frogs, ducklings, and even small mammals.

Herons have long, sharp beaks and strong necks, which they use to hunt fish and frogs.

COOL FORESTS

Animals who live deep in the forest are used to surviving both warm, summer days and cold, snowy winter ones.

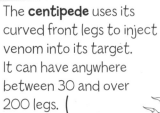

The **centipede** uses its curved front legs to inject venom into its target. It can have anywhere between 30 and over 200 legs.

Squirrels prepare for cold, snowy winters by hiding food, such as nuts, in the ground.

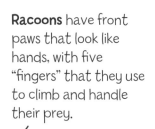

Racoons have front paws that look like hands, with five "fingers" that they use to climb and handle their prey.

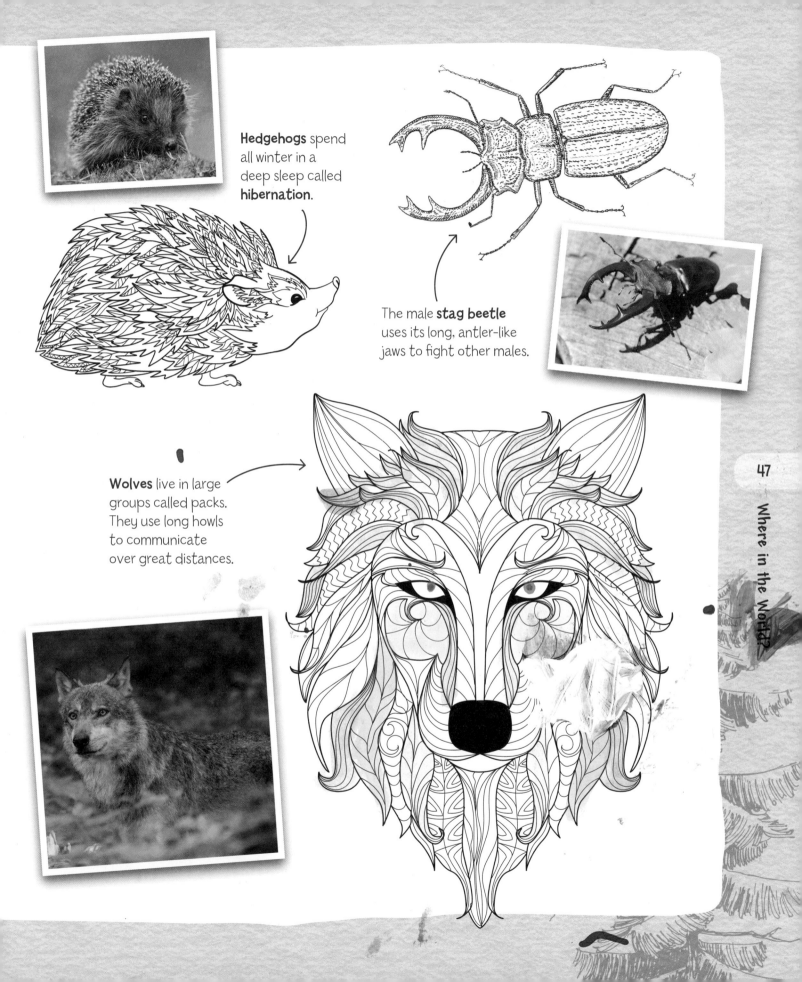

Hedgehogs spend all winter in a deep sleep called **hibernation**.

The male **stag beetle** uses its long, antler-like jaws to fight other males.

Wolves live in large groups called packs. They use long howls to communicate over great distances.

GIANT GRASSLANDS

These huge spaces in Africa are home to an incredible variety of animals—from mighty elephants to tiny termites.

Male lions have long, bushy manes that grow around their faces. They are the only type of big cat where the male looks strikingly different from the female.

The pattern on each **giraffe** is unique—no two animals look the same.

Termites live in colonies of up to 5 million and build mounds that can reach 5 m (17 ft) high!

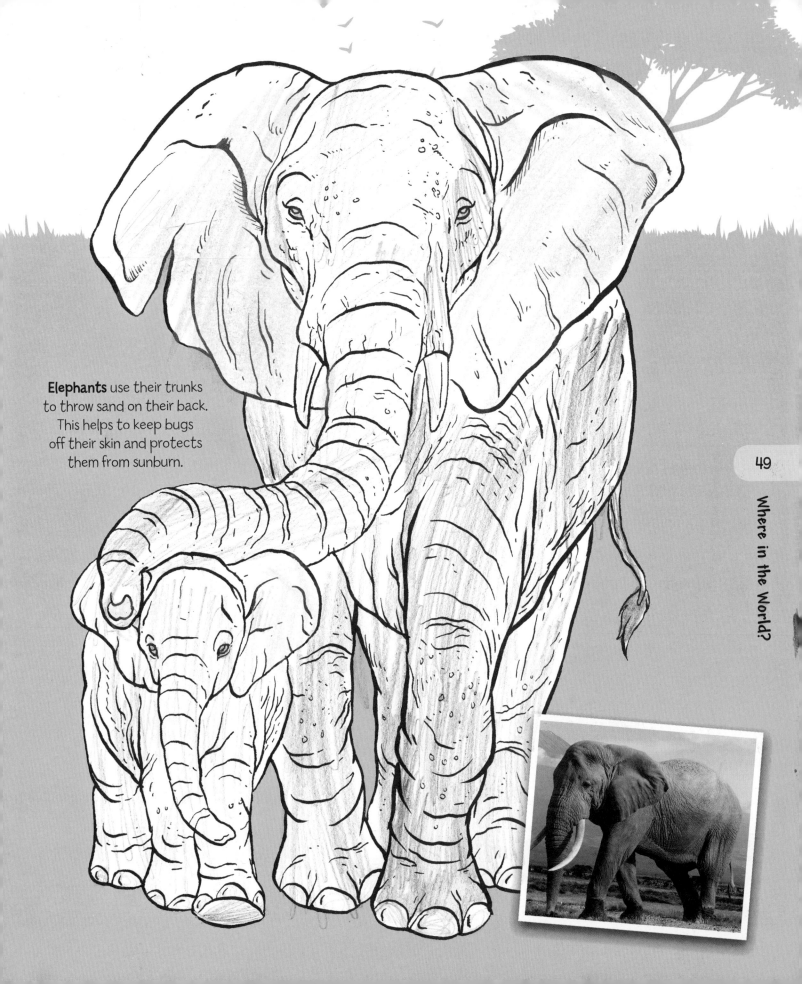

Elephants use their trunks to throw sand on their back. This helps to keep bugs off their skin and protects them from sunburn.

HIGH AND HIDDEN

While mountains are exposed to some of the harshest weather, animals who make their homes in caves are shielded from the gales, ice, and snow. Their challenge is to survive in a damp, dark environment.

In dark caves, the **bat** uses its ears to pick up sounds and figure out where its next meal is hiding.

The **snow leopard** lives in the vast, towering mountains of Central Asia. Its thick fur protects it from the frost and snow.

The **Andean condor** is the world's largest bird of prey. Its outstretched wings measure 3 m (10 ft) across.

Red pandas live in bamboo forests high up in the mountains. During especially cold winters, they go into a deep sleep for hours at a time to save energy.

Mountain gorillas can stand up to 1.8 m (6 ft) tall and can look fearsome, but they are peaceful creatures that only eat fruit, roots, and tree bark.

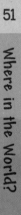

EYE SEE YOU

The animals in this chapter have highly trained senses to help them communicate, find food, and stay safe. First off, get ready for some creatures with incredible eyesight!

Cuttlefish can see types of light that are invisible to humans. Based on what they see, their skin tone changes, so they blend in with their surroundings.

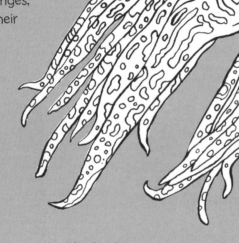

Mantis shrimp use an astoundingly fast and devastating punch to defend and attack. They manage to land a precise blow every time, thanks to their amazing eyesight.

Pigeons are often used in sea rescue missions. Their strong eyesight means that they can locate shipwreck survivors incredibly quickly while flying over the ocean.

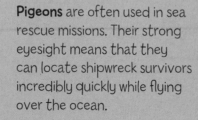

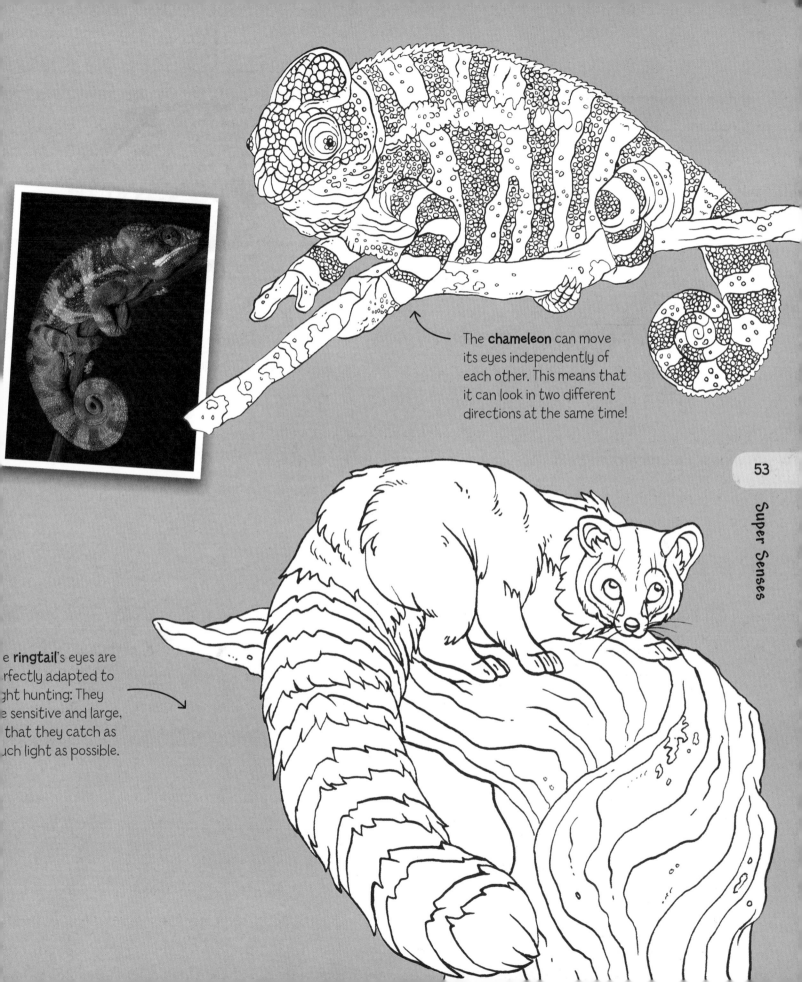

The **chameleon** can move its eyes independently of each other. This means that it can look in two different directions at the same time!

e **ringtail**'s eyes are rfectly adapted to ght hunting: They e sensitive and large, that they catch as uch light as possible.

LISTEN UP!

Whether they use it to stay safe from predators or to hunt successfully, these animals are very good listeners ...

Each kind of **frog** (such as this splendid leaf frog) has eardrums that are particularly good at picking up the sound of its own species' call.

The **bat-eared fox** uses its oversized ears to pick up the noises made by its insect prey in the soil.

Caracals use 20 muscles to move their ears precisely and independently of each other. The tufts may also help catch sounds.

The hearing of the **harvest mouse** is so sensitive, it can hear leaves rustling up to 7 m (23 ft) away.

Boreal owls hunt at night. They use their exceptional hearing to precisely locate their rodent targets. Their ears are on either side of their head, tucked away under their feathers.

SNIFFING OUT DANGER

Smelling prey or trouble coming is what these creatures do best. And unlike humans, they aren't always limited to using their noses, either. Prepare to be amazed!

Mosquitoes are able to smell carbon dioxide—the gas that humans and animals breathe out. This helps them quickly locate a source of blood!

An **albatross** can pick up a scent trail and follow it for up to 20 km (12 mi) to find food. It even manages to do this in strong ocean winds.

The **great white shark** has such a strong sense of smell that it can detect a single drop of blood—even if it's floating in 10 billion drops of water!

Lions use a powerful organ (Jacobson's organ) that sits in the roof of their mouths. They pick up smells with this organ by opening their mouths and grimacing.

Some male **moths** can smell a female that is up to 11 km (6 mi) away by using their **antennae**.

Rattlesnakes have a Jacobson's organ (see above), too. They transfer scents to it by flicking their forked tongues in and out of their mouths.

A MATTER OF TASTE

For these animals, the sense of taste is incredibly important. They first need smell, however, to find food and figure out whether it is edible and if it has the right nutrients.

When a **rabbit** grazes, it puts its 17,000 **taste buds** to important use—it can tell immediately which plants are toxic and which ones are not.

Butterflies taste with their feet! They can stand on leaves to see whether their young will be able to eat them.

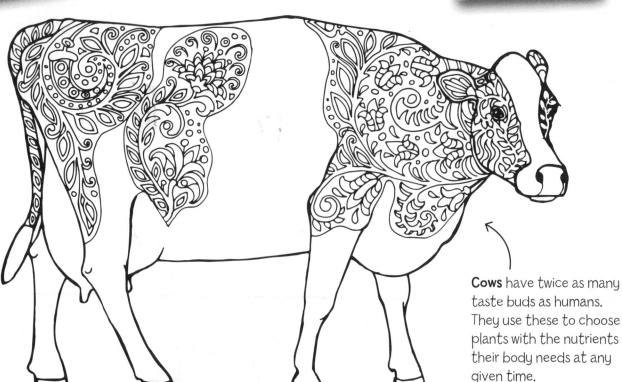

Cows have twice as many taste buds as humans. They use these to choose plants with the nutrients their body needs at any given time.

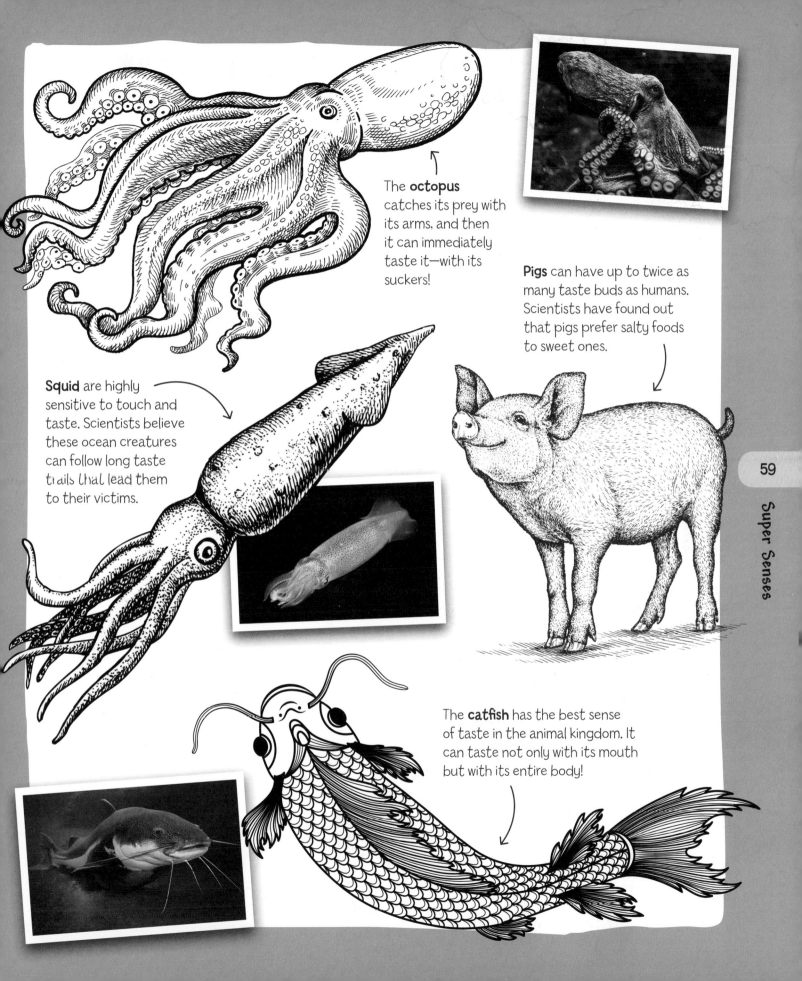

The **octopus** catches its prey with its arms, and then it can immediately taste it—with its suckers!

Pigs can have up to twice as many taste buds as humans. Scientists have found out that pigs prefer salty foods to sweet ones.

Squid are highly sensitive to touch and taste. Scientists believe these ocean creatures can follow long taste trails that lead them to their victims.

The **catfish** has the best sense of taste in the animal kingdom. It can taste not only with its mouth but with its entire body!

HOW TOUCHING!

A well-developed sense of touch doesn't just protect animals from predators. Those that live in groups use this sense to gather and travel together.

Locusts have tiny hairs on their legs. When these hairs sense fellow locusts close by, the animals start to form a swarm.

Crabs have small hairs on their body that detect currents and vibrations. They use this as a warning system for predators.

This **raft spider** doesn't use a web to hunt. Instead, it sits by the water's edge with its front legs resting on the water. As soon as its victim approaches, it senses the vibrations and pounces.

The **mole** mostly lives underground. It uses its sensitive nose to feel for prey in the dark soil.

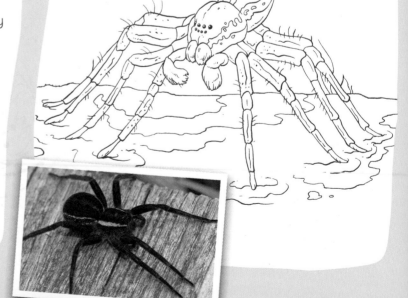

Fish can detect changes in water pressure using receptors that run along the sides of their body. This helps them locate prey and form huge shoals.

Many animals, including all species of cat, use whiskers to make sense of their surroundings. These fine, sturdy hairs extend beyond the body of the animal and help it find its way in the dark.

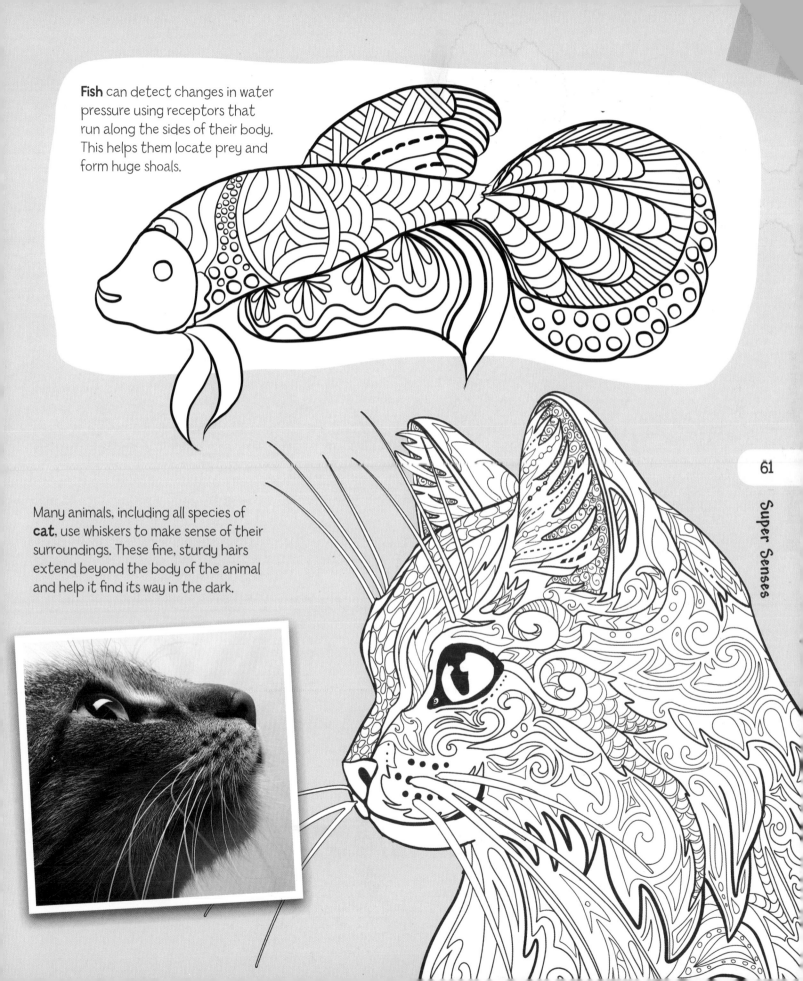

MYSTERIOUS ECHOES

Echolocating animals send out calls and listen to the echoes that bounce back from objects near them. They cleverly use these echoes to identify their surroundings.

The **shrew** echolocates by producing high-pitched "twittering" sounds. It uses the information to find hiding spots.

Oilbirds live and breed in caves. They use echolocation to navigate the dark areas and find their nests.

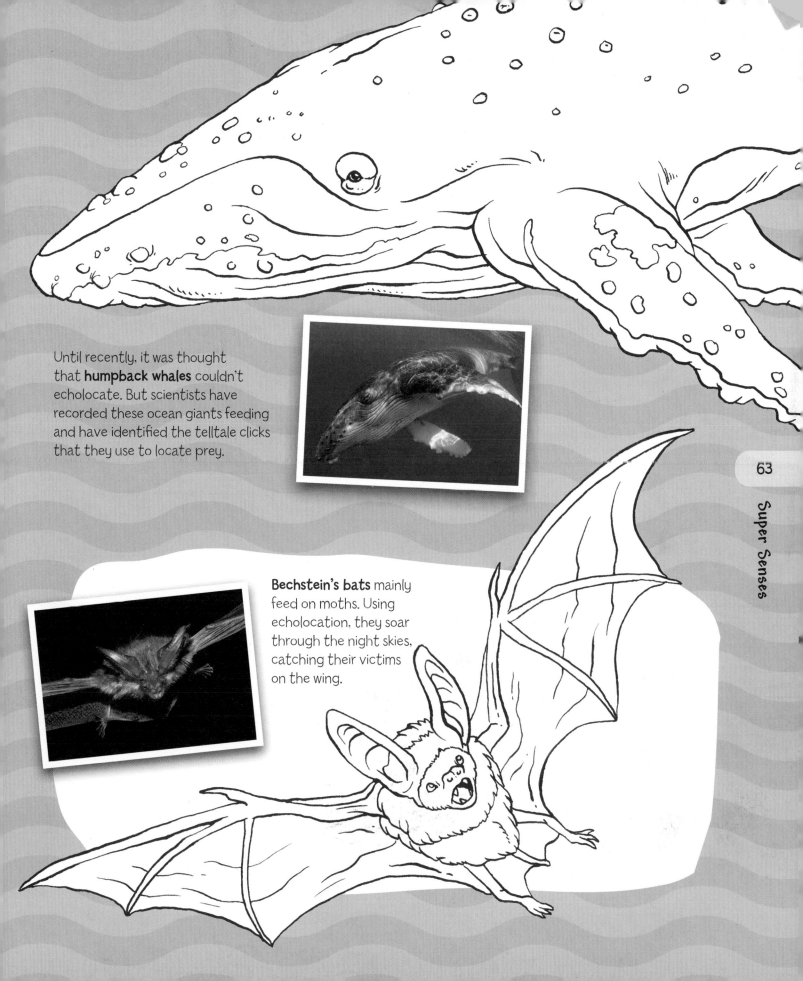

Until recently, it was thought that **humpback whales** couldn't echolocate. But scientists have recorded these ocean giants feeding and have identified the telltale clicks that they use to locate prey.

Bechstein's bats mainly feed on moths. Using echolocation, they soar through the night skies, catching their victims on the wing.

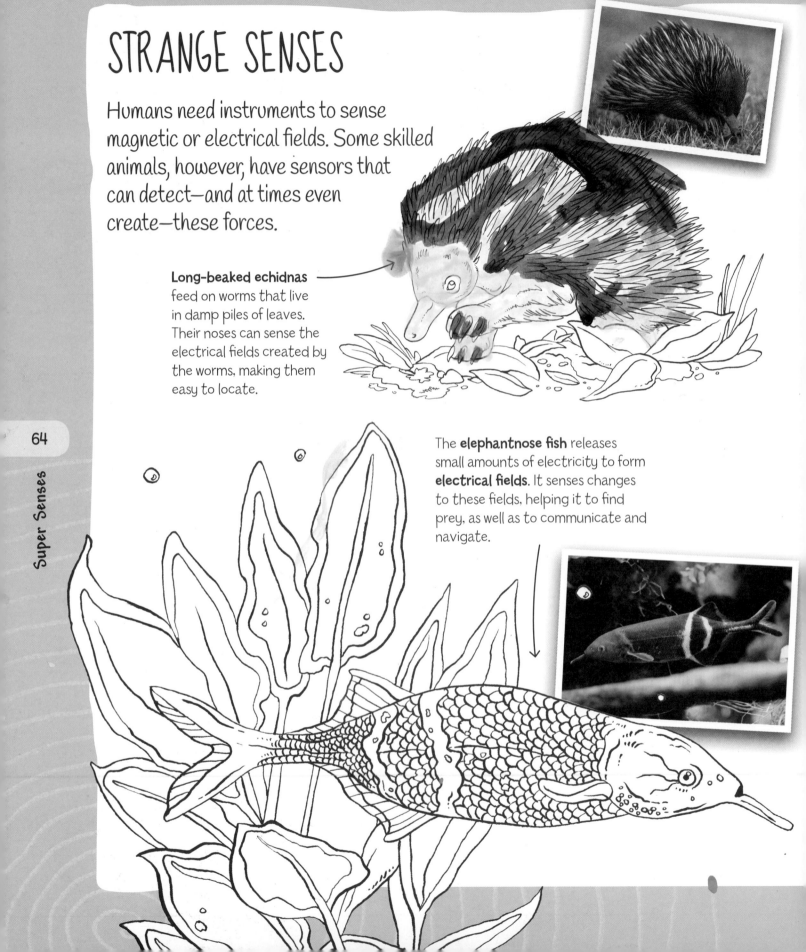

STRANGE SENSES

Humans need instruments to sense magnetic or electrical fields. Some skilled animals, however, have sensors that can detect—and at times even create—these forces.

Long-beaked echidnas feed on worms that live in damp piles of leaves. Their noses can sense the electrical fields created by the worms, making them easy to locate.

The **elephantnose fish** releases small amounts of electricity to form **electrical fields**. It senses changes to these fields, helping it to find prey, as well as to communicate and navigate.

Scientists believe that **honeybees** may be able to detect magnetic fields. This could help them to travel around and return to good sources of food.

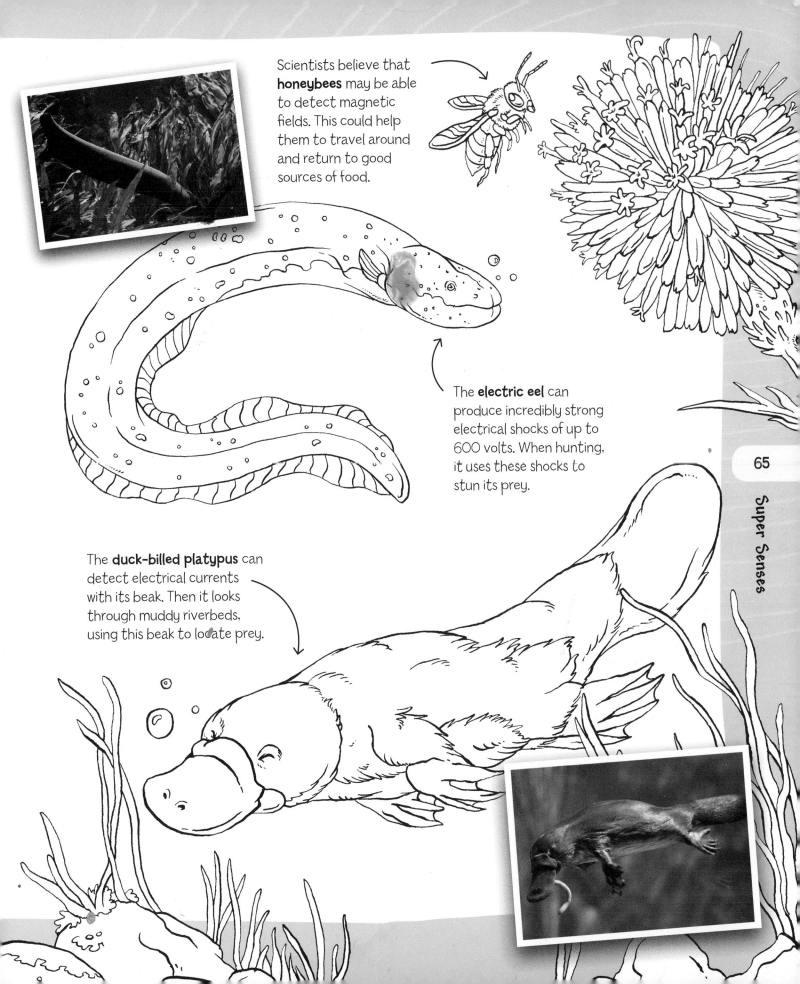

The **electric eel** can produce incredibly strong electrical shocks of up to 600 volts. When hunting, it uses these shocks to stun its prey.

The **duck-billed platypus** can detect electrical currents with its beak. Then it looks through muddy riverbeds, using this beak to locate prey.

FURRY FRIENDS

All mammals have fur—they may not have it all over their bodies, like a horse, but even whales have a few bristles! These hairs protect animals and, through grooming, help them to bond with each other.

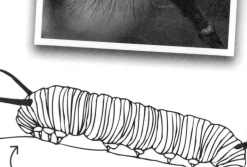

Poodles were once working dogs. They were trained to fetch ducks from the water during a hunt. Their thick fur kept them warm during their chilly swims.

Caterpillars don't have "real" fur, but some have bristles that they use to defend themselves. Add bristles to this caterpillar!

Cats use special sensory hairs and whiskers to pick up on vibrations and air currents.

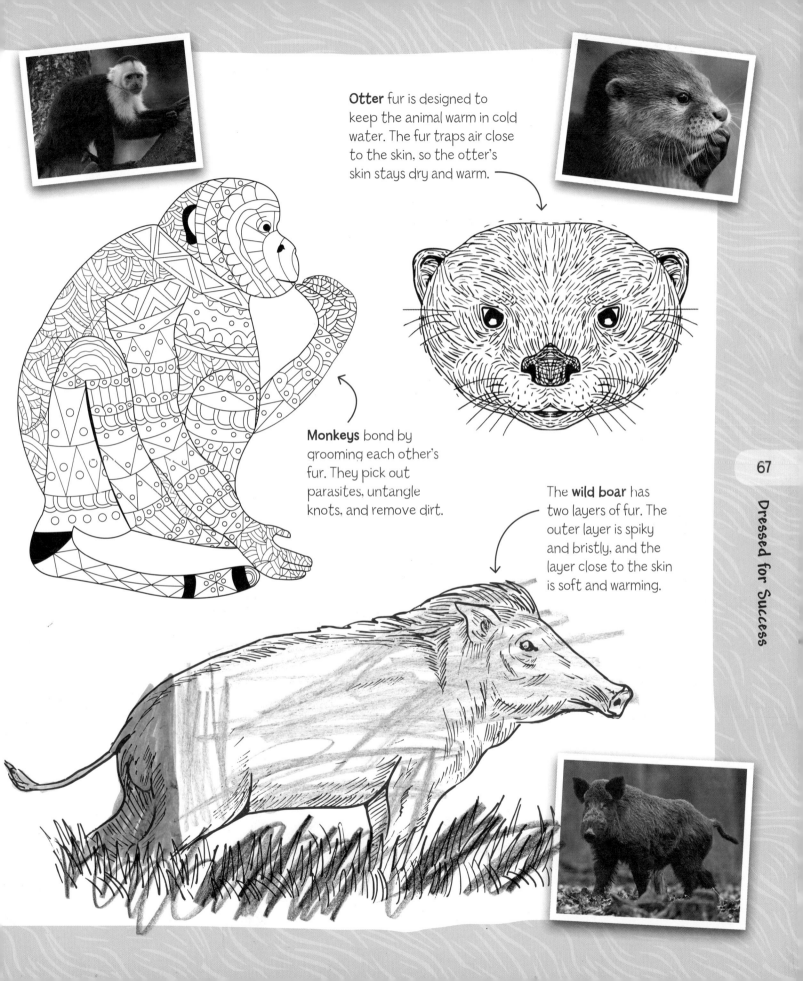

Otter fur is designed to keep the animal warm in cold water. The fur traps air close to the skin, so the otter's skin stays dry and warm.

Monkeys bond by grooming each other's fur. They pick out parasites, untangle knots, and remove dirt.

The **wild boar** has two layers of fur. The outer layer is spiky and bristly, and the layer close to the skin is soft and warming.

SCALING UP

Scales are small, closely set plates that are often covered in the same material as our nails and hair. Scales protect the animal but still allow it to move around freely.

The wings of **butterflies** are made up of tiny scales that shimmer in the sunlight. This makes it easier to be seen by mating partners.

Chameleons can change their scales to match their surroundings.

Snakes are covered in overlapping scales. Every time they grow, they shed the outer layer.

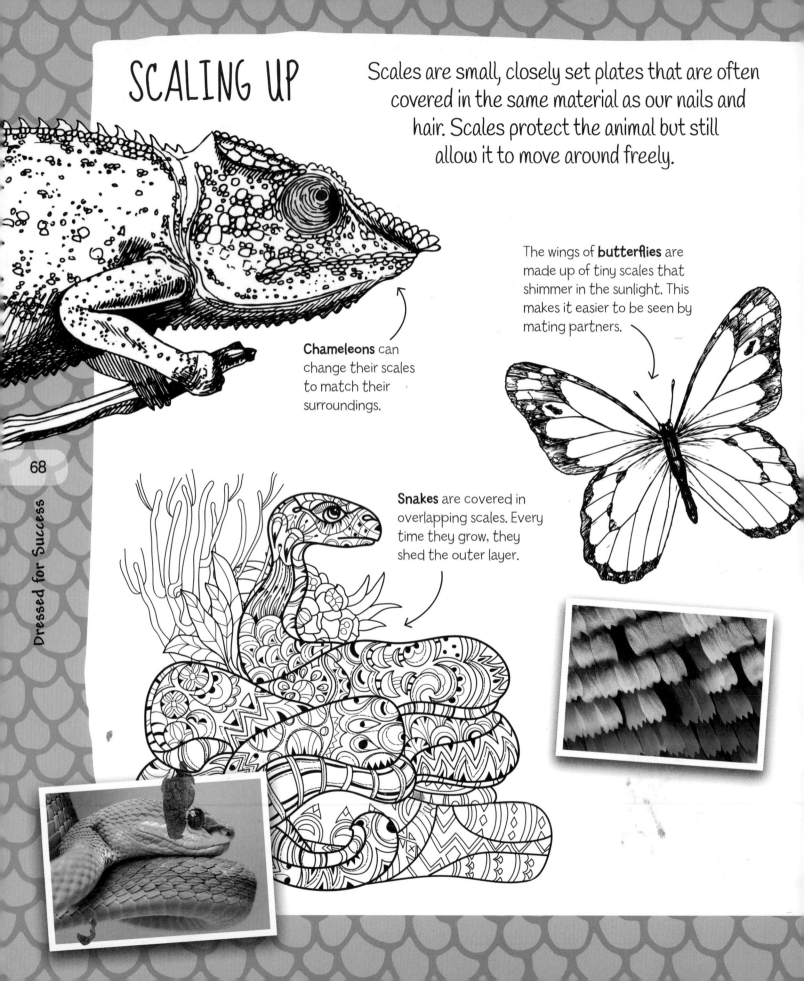

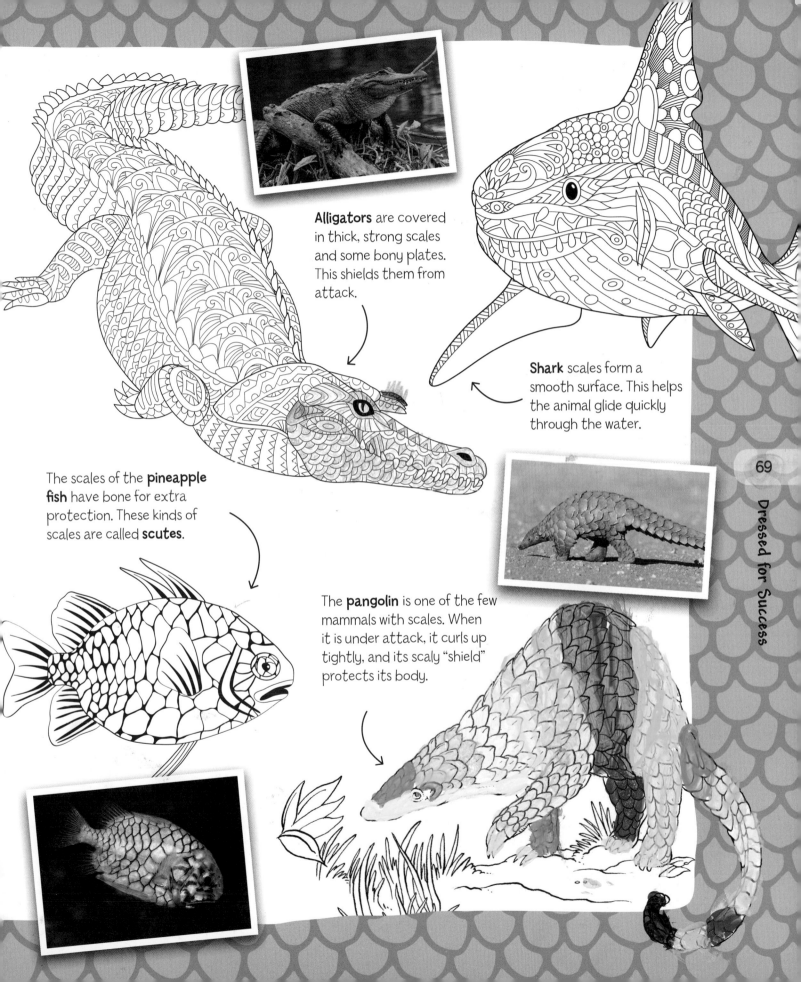

Alligators are covered in thick, strong scales and some bony plates. This shields them from attack.

Shark scales form a smooth surface. This helps the animal glide quickly through the water.

The scales of the **pineapple fish** have bone for extra protection. These kinds of scales are called **scutes**.

The **pangolin** is one of the few mammals with scales. When it is under attack, it curls up tightly, and its scaly "shield" protects its body.

POINTED PRICKLES

Some creatures have developed spiky, sharp spines and prickles. These scare off predators and keep the animal safe.

Porcupine spines are hollow. The animal shakes them to create a rustling sound, warning attackers to back off.

Some **sea urchins** use their spines for feeding, movement, and to defend themselves.

When under atack, some **tenrec** young can rub their quills together, which makes a sound. Their parents can hear this and rush to protect them!

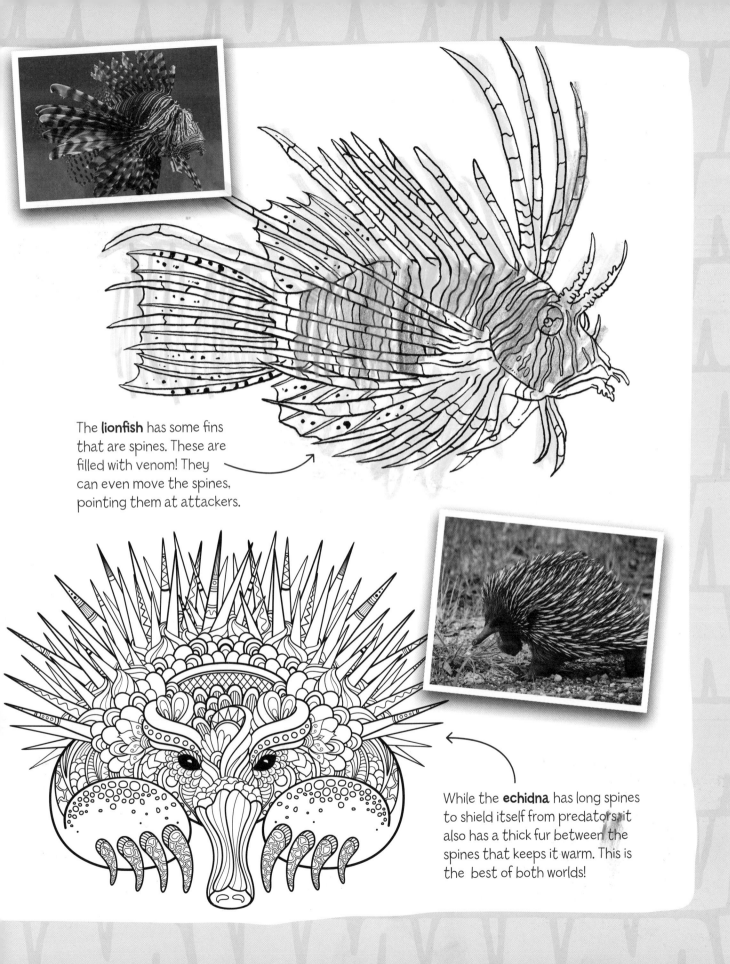

The **lionfish** has some fins that are spines. These are filled with venom! They can even move the spines, pointing them at attackers.

While the **echidna** has long spines to shield itself from predators, it also has a thick fur between the spines that keeps it warm. This is the best of both worlds!

FLUTTERING FEATHERS

Feathers are not just the reason birds can fly. They can waterproof, decorate, and warm their owners, and they come in many shapes and sizes.

Swallows migrate between Europe and South Africa every year. They fly up to 320 km (200 mi) per day. Their feathers give them the perfect outline for long-distance flying.

Black swans use their beak to cover feathers in an oil, making them water-repellent.

The **crowned crane** sports an impressive straw-like, golden "crown" on its head. It is made up of stiff feather **shafts**.

Curlews nest on the grassy ground. Their spotted feathers help them blend into their surroundings and hide from predators.

When **chicks** hatch, they are covered in fluffy down feathers. They only grow flight feathers when they are a little older.

Flamingo feathers are a striking pink because of the food they eat. A change in diet means their feathers turn white!

The **cormorant** catches its food underwater. Its feathers are designed to soak up water, so that the bird can dive as deep as possible.

THE SKIN THEY'RE IN

Skin is stretchy and soft, making it a perfect covering for a body. It has many layers, which can be thin and sensitive or thick and tough.

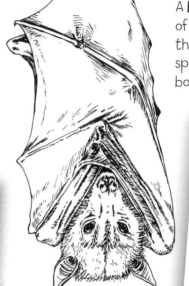

A **bat**'s wing is made of thin, leathery skin that is stretched to span the animals's long, bony digits.

The skin of **mandrill** faces forms distinctive features that are slightly different for each animal. This makes each face unique and helps them to identify each other.

The skin of the **moray eel** is covered in mucus that protects it from parasites. The mucus of some moray eels is toxic.

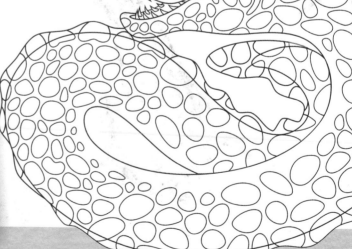

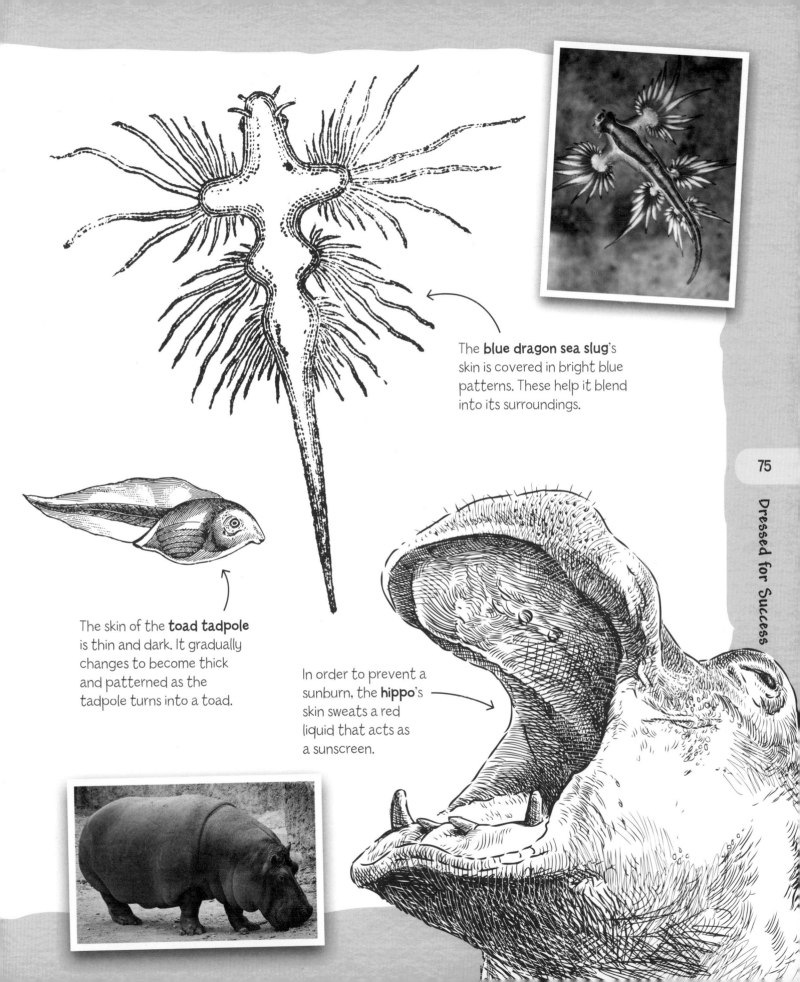

The **blue dragon sea slug**'s skin is covered in bright blue patterns. These help it blend into its surroundings.

The skin of the **toad tadpole** is thin and dark. It gradually changes to become thick and patterned as the tadpole turns into a toad.

In order to prevent a sunburn, the **hippo**'s skin sweats a red liquid that acts as a sunscreen.

OUTSIDE IN

Many animals don't have bones that give their bodies shape and stability. Instead, they have coverings called exoskeletons that encase their soft bodies.

The **centipede**'s body is cased in an exoskeleton made of cuticle. It is divided into segments, which each have a pair of legs attached.

Snails have skin that needs to stay moist. On warm days, they retreat into their shells to avoid drying out.

Nautilus shells are divided into chambers. By filling each chamber with air or water, the nautilus can control whether it floats or dives.

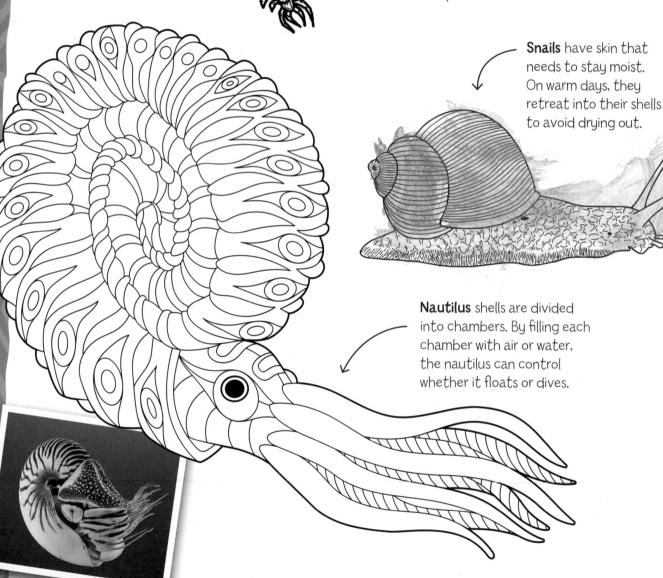

The shell of the **tortoise** is heavy and incredibly hard. When the animal tucks its legs and head into it, it is perfectly protected.

When **spiders** grow, they need to shed their old, small exoskeleton to reveal a larger one.

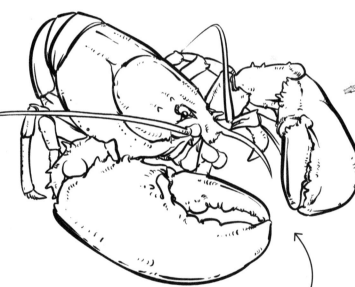

The **lobster**'s exoskeleton not only protects it—it forms huge claws that can weigh up to half of the lobster's entire body weight!

SHOWING OFF

Often in nature, male animals have developed amazing forms of display. Their appearance can show that they are powerful, in top health, or a good choice of mate.

Male **lions** have a thick, bushy mane around their neck. The older the lion, the darker the mane. They use it to appear bigger to enemies, impress females, and protect their necks during a fight.

Mandrills display a range of bright reds and blues on their faces and bottoms. The brighter they are, the more dominant or excited the baboon is.

The **Palawan peacock-pheasant** fans out and raises up its splended tail feathers, so that it can attract females.

During mating season, male **red-headed rock agamas** will change dramatically. Their scales turn from brown tones to bright red, blue, and sometimes yellow to attract a mate.

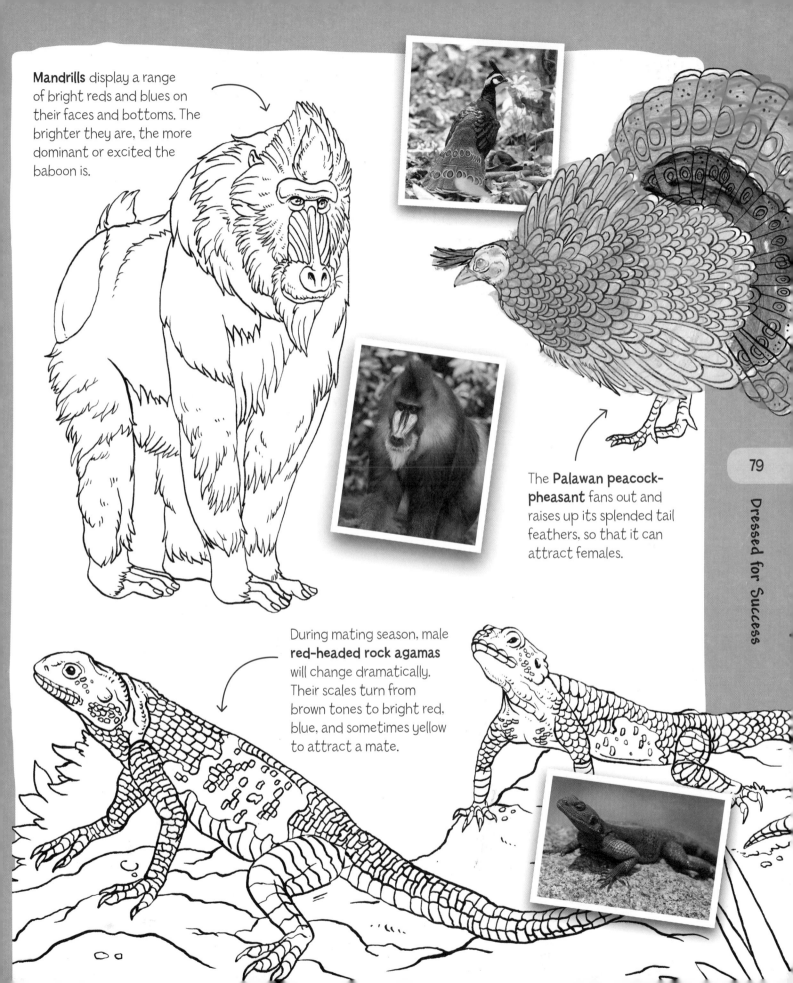

COPYCRITTERS

Although many creatures have strong protection against predators, some of those who don't have developed a smart solution: They *look* like they do.

The **clearwing moth** doesn't really look like a moth at all. With its clear wings and yellow-and-black stripes, it looks more like an animal that stings if attacked—a **wasp**.

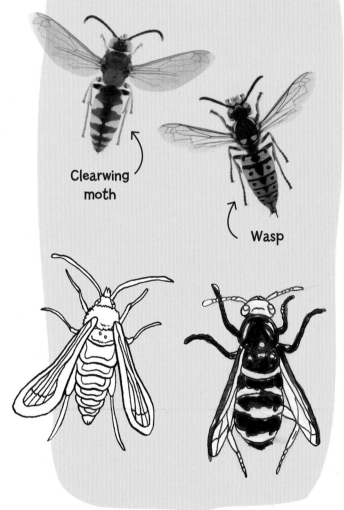

Clearwing moth

Wasp

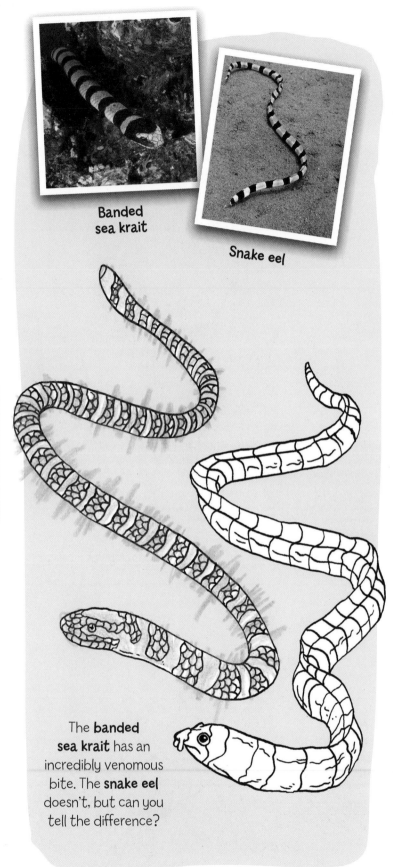

Banded sea krait

Snake eel

The **banded sea krait** has an incredibly venomous bite. The **snake eel** doesn't, but can you tell the difference?

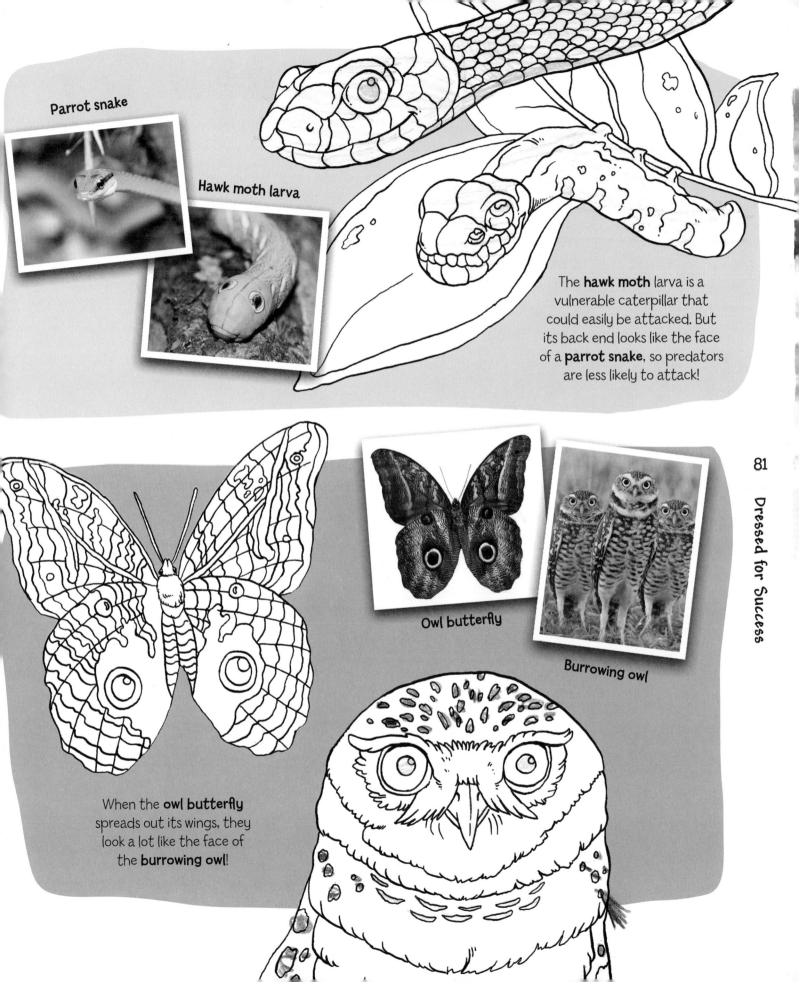

Parrot snake

Hawk moth larva

The **hawk moth** larva is a vulnerable caterpillar that could easily be attacked. But its back end looks like the face of a **parrot snake**, so predators are less likely to attack!

Owl butterfly

Burrowing owl

When the **owl butterfly** spreads out its wings, they look a lot like the face of the **burrowing owl**!

DARING DISGUISES

Blending into the surroundings or changing appearance is a great way to hide from attackers. See how well these animals hide in plain sight!

When the **common potoo** rests, it does so on tree stumps. With its mottled feathers and upright, still position, it looks like it is part of the tree!

Decorator spider crabs do as their names says: They decorate themselves! The crabs pile items on their back that help them blend into their surroundings.

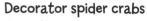

When sitting on a plant stem, the backs of **thorn bugs** make them look as if they actually are a plant's spiky thorns!

The **long-nosed butterfly fish** has a big, black dot on one of its back fins. It looks like a huge eye, while its actual eye blends in with its face.

The **scarce silver-lines moth** is a master of disguise. Its wings are green with pale lines that make them look like a leaf.

The **tiger's** stripes help it blend in while it prowls through the tall grass.

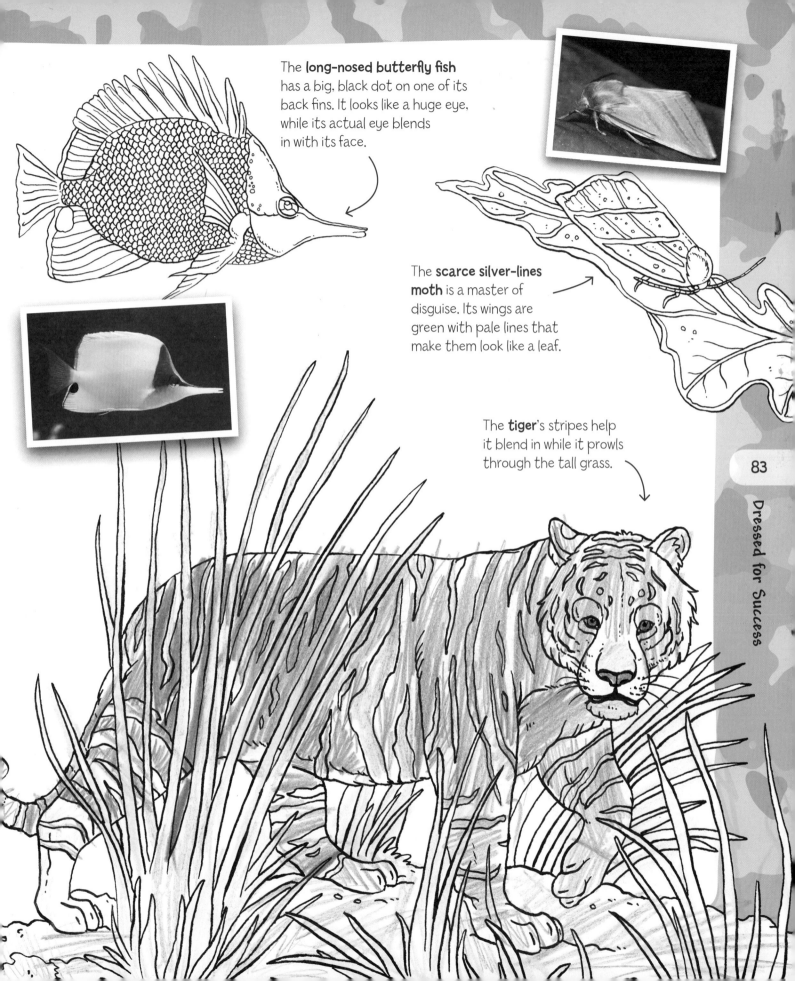

ON THE FARM

Humans have been keeping animals on farms for thousands of years—mainly for meat, wool, eggs, and milk. You may have visited a farm and spotted these animals, but how much do you know about them?

Geese were first tamed and kept by humans in Egypt over 3,000 years ago.

When given a name, **goats** will remember it and come if called.

Pigs have an excellent sense of smell—using their snout, they can find food that is in the ground.

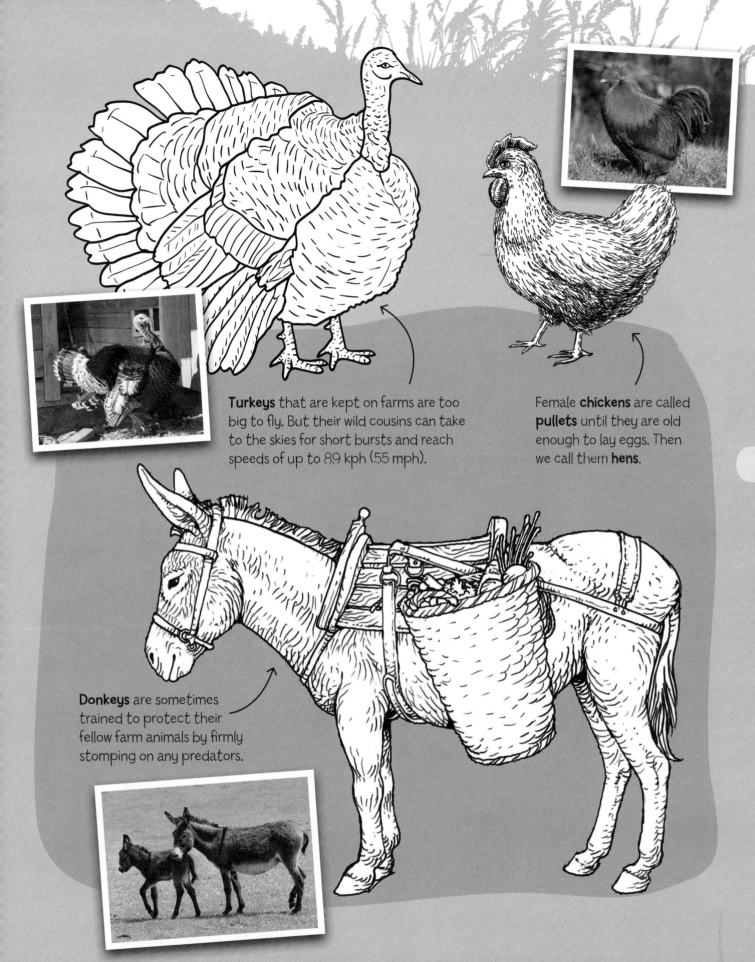

Turkeys that are kept on farms are too big to fly. But their wild cousins can take to the skies for short bursts and reach speeds of up to 89 kph (55 mph).

Female **chickens** are called **pullets** until they are old enough to lay eggs. Then we call them **hens**.

Donkeys are sometimes trained to protect their fellow farm animals by firmly stomping on any predators.

HOOFING AROUND

In many countries, large, hoofed, herding animals are kept on farms that cover vast landscapes. We also call these places ranches.

Watusi cattle have some of the largest horns of any cattle. One record-holder's horns each weighed more than 45 kg (100 lb)!

The **buffalo**'s coat is so thick and insulating that if snow settles on it, it doesn't melt.

There are over 400 different kinds of **horses**, including short ones called **ponies**. The smallest ponies measure 76 cm (30 in) from ground to shoulder.

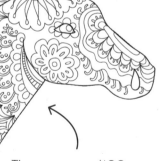

Llamas originally come from South America and are related to camels.

Cattle, such as **dairy cows**, are able to bring half-digested grass back into their mouths. They then rechew it, so that the body can break it down easier.

Sheep mothers (**ewes**) recognize the bleating of their lambs if they wander too far away or get lost in the flock.

ALL IN A DAY'S WORK

There is a long tradition of humans training animals to help them with work that they cannot do on their own.

In some cities, **hawks** are trained to guard buildings. They keep them free from smaller birds, such as pigeons, when they become pests.

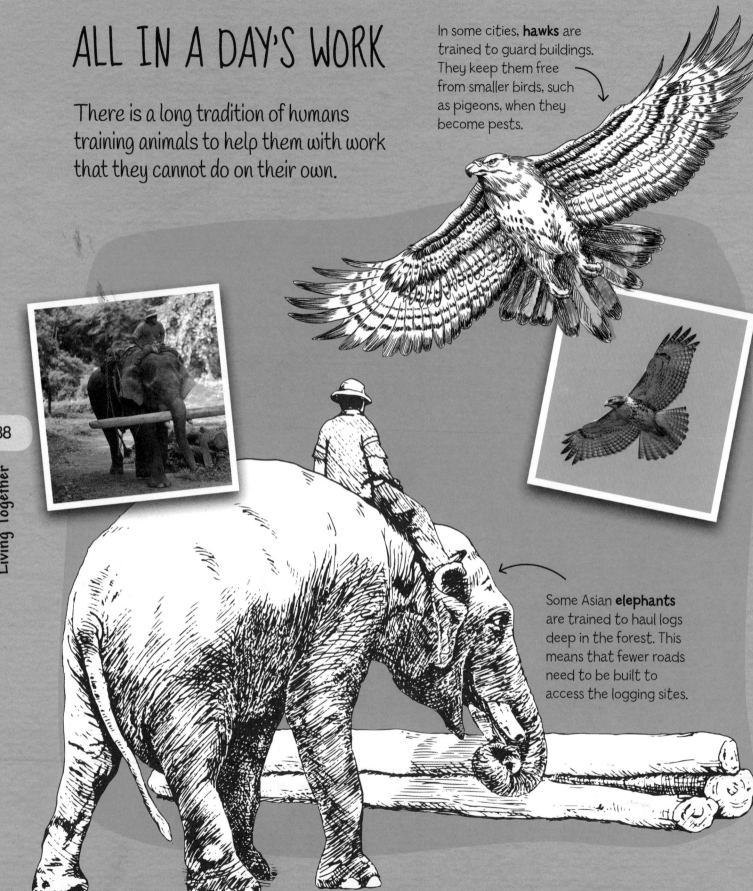

Some Asian **elephants** are trained to haul logs deep in the forest. This means that fewer roads need to be built to access the logging sites.

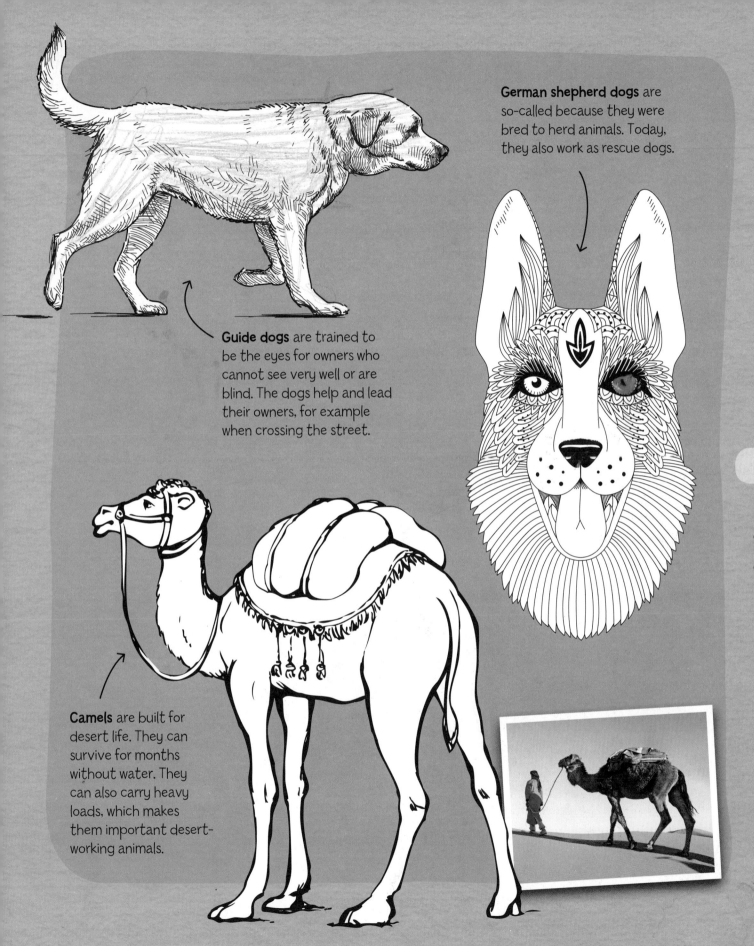

German shepherd dogs are so-called because they were bred to herd animals. Today, they also work as rescue dogs.

Guide dogs are trained to be the eyes for owners who cannot see very well or are blind. The dogs help and lead their owners, for example when crossing the street.

Camels are built for desert life. They can survive for months without water. They can also carry heavy loads, which makes them important desert-working animals.

Living Together

ADORABLE PETS

Do you have a pet? Humans all over the world share their homes with animals and form close bonds with them. Here are a few of the most popular!

Guinea pigs are neither pigs, nor are they from Guinea. They are small rodents that originally came from the Andes in South America.

Hamsters have expanding cheeks that they use to store large amounts of food. Once their cheeks are filled, they find a quiet spot to eat.

Budgies are a kind of parrot. In some cases, it is possible to teach them to say a few words!

We keep many different types of **rabbits** as pets. They vary hugely in appearance and size—the smallest pet rabbits weigh about 1 kg (2 lb), the largest around 22.5 kg (50 lb)!

Sharpen your pencils! **Zebra finch** males manage to sport a lot of bright shades and patterns. Their beaks are perfect for opening seeds.

Wild **green iguanas** live in the rain forests of South America. These lounging lizards can reach lengths of up to 1.8 m (6 ft)!

91

Living Together

AT THE ZOO

Some animals are kept in zoos, where we can visit and learn about them. Many zoos work to protect animals in the wild, too.

Macaque monkeys have cheek pouches that can hold as much food as their stomachs!

Tapirs are great swimmers and often dive deep to feed on water plants.

The female **hornbill** lays her eggs in a hollow tree trunk. She seals herself in, leaving just a tiny slit through which her mate feeds her.

Kiwis are flightless birds with wings that are hidden and only 3 cm (1 in) long!

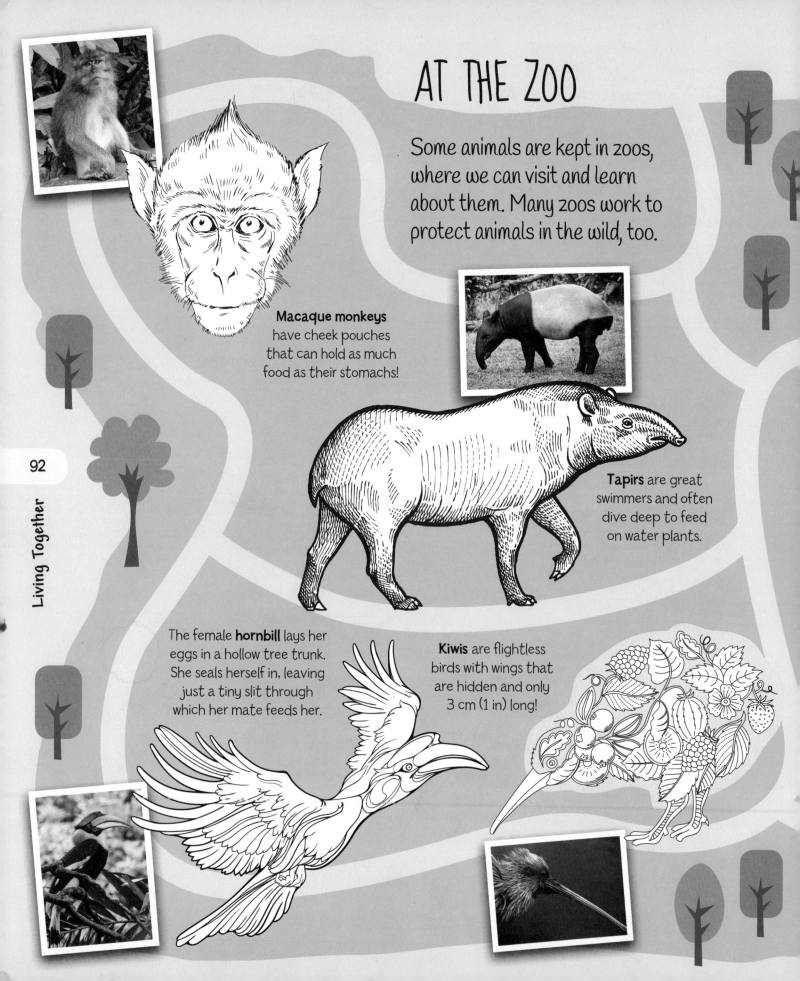

The **California sea lion**'s body is adapted to diving deep in cold ocean water. It has a thick layer of fat under its skin called blubber, which keeps it warm.

Male **ring-tailed lemurs** have "stink fights"—they smear their tails with a smelly scent and wave them in each other's face.

In the hot sun, the **black rhinoceros** will cover itself in mud. This protects its skin from sunburn and bugs.

IN THE CITY

When cities grow, living space for animals is taken away. So some animals have found new homes—in our houses and streets!

Attracted by the warmth of the city, flocks of up to one million **starlings** stop off in Rome while migrating south.

Rats can be found anywhere that humans live. They will eat almost anything and often make their homes in sewers.

In Mumbai, India, **jaguars** are a regular sight. They hunt for food at night and live peacefully alongside humans.

The **parakeet** is a type of parrot that usually lives in tropical regions. However, a growing population is now at home in London, UK.

North American **elks** often share space with humans, especially in the towns of the Rocky Mountains, such as Banff in Canada.

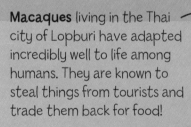

Macaques living in the Thai city of Lopburi have adapted incredibly well to life among humans. They are known to steal things from tourists and trade them back for food!

INDEX